SHE'S BEST OF SHOW . . . IN SOLVING MURDERS

My name is Holly Winter. In the week before my birth, two of my parents' golden retrievers produced a total of seventeen puppies. I was number eighteen. I'm lucky not to be "Buck's Little Lady" or "Marissa's Winsome Miss." When I graduated from grammar school, my father told everyone that I'd finally got my C.D., which, in case you hadn't guessed, is an obedience title. He was proud of me then, and he's still proud of me, partly because I haven't yet developed canine hip dysplasia.

My involvement in Dr. Stanton's death was also my parents' fault. If I'd been brought up to have a normal attitude about adopting a dead man's dog, I'd never have tried to find Rowdy's AKC registration papers. But, then, I'd also be the kind of person who'd feed supermarket dog chow instead of Eukanuba, and no one would ever have known who killed the old man . . .

Dog Lover's Mysteries by Susan Conant

A NEW LEASH ON DEATH
DEAD AND DOGGONE
A BITE OF DEATH

A NEW LEASH ON DEATH

SUSAN CONANT

CHARTER/DIAMOND BOOKS, NEW YORK

A NEW LEASH ON DEATH

A Charter/Diamond Book/published by arrangement with the author

PRINTING HISTORY
Charter/Diamond edition/September 1990

ISBN: 1-55773-385-6

Charter/Diamond Books are published by The Berkley Publishing Group, 200 Madison Avenue, New York, New York 10016.
The name "CHARTER/DIAMOND" and its logo are trademarks belonging to Charter Communications, Inc.

PRINTED IN THE UNITED STATES OF AMERICA

10 9 8 7 6 5 4 3

For Carter,
who made it possible

Acknowledgments

For technical assistance, I am grateful to my Alaskan malamute, Frostfield Arctic Natasha, C.D.

Special thanks to Roger Peduzzi, D.V.M., and James Dalsimer, M.D., for advice on medical matters. Any errors are mine alone.

Because the New England Dog Training Club meets in the Cambridge Armory on Thursday nights, it is especially important to point out that the characters and the dog training club in this novel are imaginary. Any resemblance to actual people or institutions is entirely coincidental.

A NEW LEASH ON DEATH

Chapter 1

MY name is Holly Winter. It's not my fault. Until I was born, my parents, or, as they always said, my sire and dam, hadn't had any practice in naming people. In the week before my birth, two of their golden retriever bitches produced a total of seventeen puppies. I was number eighteen. I'm lucky not to be "Buck's Little Lady" or "Marissa's Winsome Miss." I've often had the feeling that a human puppy must have been a surprise to Buck and Marissa. They must have been stunned when I began to utter words. Buck still considers speech to be some peculiarly advanced form of barking. When I graduated from grammar school, he told everyone that I'd finally got my C.D., which, in case you hadn't guessed, is an obedience title, Companion Dog. With my high school diploma, I became a Companion Dog Excellent, and when I got my B.A. in journalism, I was Marissa's fifth Utility Dog. Buck was proud of me then, and he's still proud of me, partly, I suspect, because I'm thirty years old and haven't yet developed canine hip dysplasia. I'm also something of a puzzle to him. Although he subscribes to *Dog's Life* and reads my column, he can't understand why I write about dogs instead of breeding them. Furthermore, he can't understand why anyone who's welcome to share his house in Maine with him and his fifteen wolf dog hybrids would choose to live in Cambridge, Massachusetts. Buck's become a little eccentric in the eight years since Marissa died.

My involvement with Dr. Stanton's death was, like my name, Buck and Marissa's fault. If I'd been brought up to have a normal attitude about adopting a dead man's dog, I'd never have tried to find Rowdy's AKC registration papers. But, then, I'd also be the kind of person who'd feed supermarket dog chow instead of Eukanuba, and I'd never insist on precision heeling, and no one would ever have known who killed the old man.

It started on a Thursday evening last November. Thursday evenings are to me what Friday nights are to Orthodox Jews. Every Thursday night between seven and ten, the Cambridge Dog Training Club holds classes in the Cambridge Armory, and, unless I happen to have a bitch in season, you'll find me there. *Bitch,* by the way, is not a dirty word. One way to spot a newcomer to the world of dogs is any hesitation about saying it. Bitches in season are bitches in heat, and, for obvious reasons, they're not welcome at dog training classes or obedience trials. In the presence of a bitch in season, the only thing an unaltered male dog obeys is the call of the wild.

To understand what happened to Dr. Stanton, you need to know a little about the Cambridge Armory. A lot of dog training clubs meet in armories because armories are large enough to hold even big beginners' classes, and also because armories are a lot nicer than schools or YMCAs about what are always called accidents. Armories, of course, don't particularly *like* accidents, either. Go to any dog training class in the world, and you'll find one rule: If your dog has an accident, you clean it up. There's another rule about accidents: Don't let your dog have any on the grounds of the armory. Armory managers are convinced that dogs have one aim in life. On the night Dr. Stanton died, I'll bet Gerry Pitts, the manager of the Cambridge Armory, checked outside at least ten times just to make sure that no handlers were exercising their dogs on the lawn.

If you're walking up to the armory from Concord Avenue, there are chain link fences on your left and right to keep you off the lawn. Just before you get to the steps of the building, there's a gate to the lawn on either side. You go through a set of glass doors to enter the front hallway. The men's room is on the left. Ahead of you is a set of swinging doors that are always open, and through the doors is the big hall where we hold classes. Really, it's a gym with a battered floor that's better for dog training than for basketball. Dogs slip on highly polished surfaces, and if there's one thing that most dogs hate, it's slipping. No dog has ever objected to the floor of the Cambridge Armory, and I keep hoping that no one ever gets the idea of refinishing it. The armory is shabby, just the way I like it.

If you show up on a Thursday night, you'll see a big group of dogs and handlers in front of you, and at the far end of the hall, separated by a stretch of portable baby gates, you'll see a small advanced class. To your left, against the wall and near the door to the armory's offices, you'll find our desk, which is, of course, a card table. The ladies' room, should you need it, is to the left of the door to the offices. All along the left side of the hall are bleachers. At the far end, on the right, beyond the small advanced class, you might notice the door that leads to a shelter for homeless men. The shelter is open only in cold weather. The men are allowed to enter the shelter at ten, when we leave, but sometimes they hang around the front door and the hallway to wait.

On that Thursday night, I was dogless and had been for about a month. My last golden, Marissa's parting gift to me, died in September, and Buck was taking his time about finding me another, mainly, I suspect, because he intended to surprise me with a wolf dog pup. Don't get me wrong. I like wolves, and I like wolf dogs as much as I like all other dogs. My only objection to Buck's current obsession is that you can't register wolf dogs with the American Kennel Club (or, as Buck says, you can't register them *yet*), and if a dog can't be registered, he can't be entered in a sanctioned obedience trial. You can train and enter him in fun matches, but I'm too much Marissa's daughter to bother training a dog I can't really show. Besides, I make my living in the dog world, and I can always use another C.D. on my résumé.

In any case, I'd volunteered to help Ray Metcalf at the desk that night because I knew that my doglessness was temporary—it always is—and I wanted to get my yearly turn out of the way. The Metcalfs breed Clumber spaniels and, to prove "Winter's rule," look nothing like their dogs. Ray and Lynne are both so tall and bony that if they were dogs, they'd be aging greyhounds. Clumber spaniels are long and low, like basset hounds, and they're supposed to look heavy. Although my hair is the color of a dark golden retriever, I bear little resemblance to any other breed of dog I've ever owned.

Ray and I were busy around seven because it was the first Thursday of the month, when a new beginners' class always starts, and we had to give people forms to fill out, collect the forms and the money, and keep the untrained dogs from mauling one another while the handlers did their paperwork. Barbara Doyle, who has German shepherds, helped us. We also checked in a few people for the Utility class that Roz runs at the far end of the hall while Vince Dragone, our head trainer, does the beginners' class.

The more advanced a dog training class is, the smaller it is. Most people originally go to dog training because they just want the dog to come when it's called. Before long, they discover that there's no "just" about it. Once beginners realize that a reliable recall isn't something you achieve in eight Pre-Novice classes, most of them quit. On that Thursday night, Vince's beginners' class had twenty-five dogs, and Roz's Utility class had three.

At eight, the beginners left, and the advanced beginners, who'd had four lessons, arrived. Ray and I checked everyone in, and Vince started his second class of the night. Hussan, his Rottweiler, was still on what's called a long down: Hussan hadn't moved since seven, and he'd be in exactly the same place until Vince released him. It takes a lot of patience to train a dog that well, and it takes an imperturbable personality to come in at seven, teach for three hours, and leave at ten looking as relaxed as if he'd been training for ten minutes.

When the club fired Margaret Robichaud and replaced her with Vince, Margaret blamed Dr. Stanton and said we were sexist, but the membership doubled. Margaret's approach—jerk on the dog's lead, and if that doesn't work, jerk harder—was going out of style, and we were all pretty tired of her gift for putting people off. She used to tell the beginners that if they weren't going to train for two hours a day, they should go home and forget it. She and Dr. Stanton were already less than friends, but he only spoke for the rest of us. We were all thrilled at the chance to hire Vince, who understands that all dogs are descended from wolves and who likes dogs the way they are.

At eight-thirty, the five members of Roz's Pre-Open class arrived. Open comes after Novice and before Utility. Novice, Open, Utility. Companion Dog, Companion Dog Excellent, Utility Dog. C.D., C.D.X., U.D. The Novice exercises, the ones for a C.D., are incredibly important, since they're the foundation of everything else, but they can bore an intelligent dog. The point of Roz's Pre-Open class was to liven things up for the dogs while giving them a head start on the Open exercises, which are fun, especially retrieving and jumping. Five people had taken Roz up on her offer to do the Pre-Open class.

The first person to check in for Roz's class that night was Steve Delaney, my vet and my lover, with India, his German shepherd. Steve's eyes are something like Siberian blue, but gentler and warmer, and his hair forms those thick waves you see along the back of a Chesapeake Bay retriever. Just in case you wondered, there's nothing ethically wrong with having an affair with your vet, especially if you've met under emotionally charged circumstances. When old Dr. Draper diagnosed Vinnie's cancer in June, I thought he'd see us through, but he retired in August. Vinnie didn't show the pain until early September, and by then, Steve had taken over the practice. After he ended Vinnie's suffering, he spent half an hour holding my hand and listening to the story of her life. My friend Rita, who's a shrink, believes in a primordial link between sex and death. That night I had a vivid dream about Steve. The next day I called to thank him—for his help with Vinnie, not for the dream—and he's been consoling me ever since.

The second to check in for Roz's class that Thursday night was Dr. Frank Stanton, one of the grand old persons of obedience training. He looked better than he had for a while. Until about a year earlier, he was living proof that if you want to stay young, forget Nautilus and Retin-A. Just keep training dogs. Lately, though, he'd been pale. When he had some color, he was an attractive man, tall, with lots of white hair and heavy glasses. That night, as usual, he was dressed more warmly than anyone else. His sweater was one of those expensive hand-knit Irish ones, and over it he wore a tweed sport coat.

A founding member of the Cambridge Dog Training Club, he was also an official in four or five other dog organizations and an unofficial historian of the American dog world. Two years earlier, when his eyesight started to fail badly, he stopped going to shows, but he never missed a class, and he was still strong enough to handle Rowdy, his Alaskan malamute. That's pretty strong. There are bigger dogs that can pull more than a malamute, but, pound for pound, an Alaskan malamute is possibly the strongest dog in the world. If you see an arctic dog with blue eyes, it's a Siberian husky, not a malamute, whose eyes are brown. Siberians are smaller and faster. (By the way, never call a Siberian a husky.) I remember wondering, when Dr. Stanton checked in that night, why Buck had decided to breed wolf dogs when he could have had a malamute. Maybe it was because he thought wolves would be easier to train. A lot of people would agree with him.

"How's Rowdy doing these days?" I asked as I returned Dr. Stanton's card. Once you get beyond the beginner's stage and join our club, you pay twenty dollars for a card that's worth six lessons. The card has the numbers 1 through 6 printed along the bottom, and whenever you check in, the person at the desk punches out a number.

"I believe that Rowdy is beginning to pull slightly less, but I may, of course, be deceiving myself," he said.

Especially with young women, he had a courtly manner. You know that Harvard accent that movie actors never get quite right? Dr. Stanton had the real thing, and for an old man, he had a young voice, thanks to a lifetime of talking to dogs. Rowdy obviously liked the accent and the voice. When Dr. Stanton said his name, he quit trying to provoke Hussan into getting up and gave Dr. Stanton a doggy grin and a tail swish. When Dr. Stanton wasn't acting courtly, he could be outright nasty to people, but he deserved every canine smile and wag he ever received.

Lynne Metcalf, with a young Clumber spaniel, also checked in for Roz's class. Lynne is so rich she doesn't have to work for a living, but she's a nice person anyway. Ron Coughlin arrived next, with Vixen, a mixed breed bitch (setter, golden, Doberman, and who knows what else), who was possibly the most intelligent dog in the club. Ron had been junior partner in Coughlin and Sons Plumbing and Heating for twenty years. Then came Diane D'Amato, with the movie star of the club, her black miniature poodle Curly, who'd just filmed a TV commercial for rawhide chew toys. One of Curly's specialties is dancing on his hind legs. He rises up on tiptoe and prances around in a circle or across the floor. He knows how to bark out an accompaniment. Don't get the idea that Diane is rich. Dogs get paid a flat fee with no residuals for commercials. Diane earns her living as the office manager of an auto body shop. Curly's work doesn't pay much, but Diane gets a kick out of seeing him on TV, and so does the rest of the club.

Dog trainers are a diverse group. About all we have in common is dogs. One of the complaints some people made about Margaret Robichaud was that she preferred the idle rich to the rest of us. I never noticed it, but, of course, she would have carefully avoided offending someone who writes for *Dog's Life.* I did notice that Margaret spent more time with purebred dogs, especially golden retrievers, than with mixed breeds, and I didn't like it. One thing that's completely out of place in obedience training is any kind of snobbery.

By eight thirty-five, Vince's advanced beginners were getting ready to work on recalls.

"You're going to tell your dog to stay," Vince was saying. "Don't use his name. Put your hand, palm down, in front of his nose. Tell him to stay, and walk to the end of your leash."

Roz's dogs were learning to stay, too, but to stay still with wooden dumbbells in their mouths. After that, they'd do jumps, which most dogs adore, and then the long down with the handlers out of sight. Dog training classes are predictable. They nearly always end with a long down because that's the last exercise at an obedience trial.

At a little after eight forty-five, I heard Roz say, right on schedule, "Handlers, down your dogs."

Downing a dog might sound a little alarming, but all it means is to tell your dog to lie down.

"Leave your dogs," she said.

Steve, Diane, and Lynne marched toward the desk, past us, and through the door to the offices. People walk funny when they're leaving their dogs or returning to them. In an obedience trial, moving your head around, brushing the hair out of your face, or making any other normal gesture might be considered a signal to the dog. You're also supposed to act natural, but hardly anybody does.

Ron and Dr. Stanton walked by the desk, too, avoiding the advanced beginners, and out through the doors to the entrance hall. After about a minute, Curly stood up, which is, of course, against the rules in a long down, and Roz called out to ask us to get Diane. Like many miniature poodles, Curly is smart and mischievous. He knows that he's supposed to stay down.

Diane was just around the corner from the desk.

"Curly's up," I told her, and she paraded indignantly back

to correct him, then left again. Curly's disobedience is one hundred percent deliberate. You can always tell when he's going to pull something cute. He starts by moving his head just a little bit back and forth. His little black eyes gleam. If he's supposed to stay down, he stands up. If he's supposed to stand still, he does a soft-shoe. Diane sometimes worries that success is spoiling him.

At about eight-fifty, Roz called out, "Handlers, return to your dogs."

Ron came in through the swinging doors, and Diane, Steve, and Lynne through the door to the offices.

"Handlers," Roz called again, smiling. Roz smiles a lot. She's about forty-five. She has short, practical gray hair, and she usually wears a T-shirt with a picture of a West Highland white terrier, of which she owns three.

This was not the first time Dr. Stanton had failed to return. He liked to wait outdoors on the front steps, and although his hearing was much better than his vision, he didn't always hear Roz.

"Rowdy knows if I haven't really left," Dr. Stanton always said. "I don't know how he knows, but he knows."

Maybe Dr. Stanton was right. Except for wagging his long-haired tail, perking up his ears, and casting his big dark eyes at the other dogs, Rowdy hadn't budged. Some people will tell you that a malamute can't be trained. They're wrong. Either they don't understand malamutes or they don't put in the time.

"Will someone get Frank?" Roz called out.

But Dr. Frank Stanton never released his beautiful dog from that long down. Frank Stanton was on the longest down of all.

Chapter 2

WHEN I went to find Dr. Stanton, Gerry Pitts, the building manager, came with me, just in case, I suppose, someone arriving early for the nine o'clock Novice class was exercising a dog on the lawn. Looking out toward Concord Avenue from the entrance hall, I noticed Hal hanging around on the sidewalk. Half of Cambridge would have recognized Hal, and quite a few people would have known his name, as I did, because he would have introduced himself while he was returning trash bags full of cans and bottles at the Broadway Supermarket or lurking around parking meters mumbling to himself. Few of the shelter's clients have faces as memorably aristocratic as Hal's, and since the night was not bitterly cold, none of the others had yet arrived.

Gerry held one of the glass doors open for me, and as I walked through, I called, "Dr. Stanton?"

"Maybe he's gone to the men's room," Gerry said. "I'll take a look."

Although the weather was not cold enough to have drawn an early crowd to the shelter, it was a little too chilly for my T-shirt and jeans, and I trotted down the walk to keep warm. Hal, who must have thought I was after him, scuttled off toward the playground that's next to the armory. In Cambridge, a homeless guy who drinks isn't necessarily paranoid if he thinks that people are after him.

"He's not there," Gerry called from the doorway, and I reversed my direction.

Gerry, on principle, scanned the lawn and must have noticed that the gate was open, the chain link gate to the right of the entrance if you're facing the building. I saw Gerry bend over, and when I heard his sick groan, I started running. Dr. Stanton lay on the lawn just inside the gate.

"I'll get Steve," I said.

Without Dr. Stanton, a D.V.M. was the closest the club came to an M.D. Besides, if you think about it, how much do M.D.s really know about medicine? All they do is specialize in the trivial diseases of one late-evolved species that threatens all the others. A D.V.M., on the other hand, has to know all about everything from avian lice to canine brucellosis, bovine petechial fever, and African horse sickness. If a vet's patients aren't watched carefully, they'll bite him or kick him, or they might even eat their young. Anyway, Steve understands heart attacks. Dogs and cats have them, and I assumed that Dr. Stanton had had one, too.

Steve was still at the far end of the hall with India and Roz and the others, and I waved to him to come to the entrance. He'd released India, but he put her on another long down. Even from the opposite end of the hall, I could see her look up at him as if she wondered whether she'd done something wrong the first time. She held her head high, kept her ears alertly pricked up, and stared at Steve. She's a big bitch, mostly black, with tan legs and a light belly, a gorgeous shepherd and a genuine one-man dog. She doesn't like to have Steve out of her sight. Me neither.

"I think Stanton's had a coronary," I said when he reached me. "He's out on the lawn. Gerry's with him."

"Get me some light," he said. He's used to emergencies.

Normally, the only light at the armory entrance comes from a couple of bulbs over the front door. I wasn't sure that there were any more outside lights. If there were, I had no idea where to find the switches, so I followed Steve outside and relayed his request to Gerry. In spite of Gerry's forty surplus pounds, the absence of hair on his head, and the multiplicity of moles on his face, I had never thought of him as ugly, but as he brushed past me, he looked almost ghoulish.

The armory has, it turns out, huge outdoor floodlights, and, of course, Gerry knew where to find the switch. When the lights came on, I could see Dr. Stanton lying on his back on the grass, with Steve kneeling next to him. That kind of light isn't flattering to anyone, except possibly Steve, but Stanton's face was hideously distorted in some way I'd never seen before. Sprawled there under the floodlight, he looked like a rag doll wearing the kind of rubber Halloween mask that sensitive Cambridge parents try to prevent their children from buying at Irwin's Toy Store.

"Call an ambulance," Steve said. "And call the police. Someone's strangled him with Rowdy's leash."

If we'd been at a show, the leash would have been lying on the floor of the armory just in back of Rowdy, but if your dog gets up and starts to take off somewhere during a class, you want that leash where you can put your hands on it when you catch him. I knew exactly what had happened. Dr. Stanton had put the leash around his neck, left Rowdy, and walked outside. He'd stood on one side of the stairs, where it's dark, or, just maybe, he'd opened the gate and stepped onto the lawn. The lawn is not prohibited unless you have your dog with you. It is assumed that handlers won't exercise themselves there. Someone must have sneaked up on him, grabbed the leash, wrapped it all the way around his neck, and yanked hard.

Back inside, I called an ambulance and the police, and while I was calling, Ray and Lynne and a couple of other people overheard me, since the pay phone's on a wall near the desk. It seemed like half a day since I'd gone to tell Dr. Stanton to release Rowdy, but it couldn't have been more than a few minutes, because Vince was just ending his class, and he's usually right on schedule.

"Everybody's got to stay here," Ray said, "and somebody's got to do something about the nine o'clock people."

I could hear the sound of voices and barking in the hall. A greasy-haired woman with a Portuguese water dog was leaning against the desk listening eagerly as she waited to check in. If you'd walked up to the armory and seen Steve and Gerry kneeling by Dr. Stanton or bending over him, and if you hadn't seen his face, you'd have assumed, as many people did, that he was one of the men from the shelter, someone like Hal, a stranger who'd passed out from alcohol or hunger. Once the police arrived, nobody would continue to assume that.

The main reason we all stayed calm is that Vince and Roz were used to ordering us around, and we were used to obeying them. People say that the hardest part of training a dog is training the owner. Roz and Vince had done a good job with all of us. After hours of obeying them when they told us "Left turn," "Right turn," "About turn," and "Halt," we were ready to form a group at the far end of the hall when Vince ordered us to gather there, and the newcomers were ready to wait at the front of the hall when Roz stood at the door and directed them. Roz and Vince's expertise came in handy in another way, too. They'd both had to deal with runaway dogs, which are a serious matter in a building as close as the armory is to the traffic of Concord Avenue and the Fresh Pond rotary. Consequently, they were both carrying leashes. When Roz had seen that Dr. Stanton was not returning, she put Rowdy on hers and tied him to one of the bleachers at the far end of the hall.

People who believe in ESP like to think that dogs and their owners have special powers of communication, but if Rowdy had received some extrasensory message from Dr. Stanton, he wasn't showing any sign of it. Even though he knew that he was tied up, I think that he still believed he was on a long down, because he was in his favorite long-down posture, belly on the floor, forelegs crossed, head resting on them, tail sticking up and waving slowly. Rowdy often looked as if he were scanning for some kind of wonderful trouble and preparing to create some if he didn't find any soon enough to suit him. All malamutes are big dogs, but, at ninety pounds, Rowdy was about five pounds heavier than he should have been. Even though wolves are rangier than malamutes and have smaller, warier eyes, all malamutes, Rowdy included, look something like wolves, especially to people who've never seen real wolves up close. There is one big difference between wolves and malamutes besides the fact that malamutes carry their tails high. A wolf wants to avoid you. A malamute wants to lap your face and roll onto his back so you'll rub his tummy, and that rub-my-tummy look is the one Rowdy gave me when he caught my eye at the far end of the armory that night. An imploring look from the glittering dark brown eyes of a beautiful dog, especially a dog that's just lost his owner, is not an easy thing to ignore.

If I had been with some other group of people, I'd probably have had to keep on talking about what had happened, but dog people understand each other. In the groups I like best, it's very common to find that everyone knows the names of all of the dogs, while only a few people know other people's names. No one minds. I'm not hurt when someone forgets my name, but I expect people to know who my dogs are. Besides, I'd already told everyone everything I knew, which, at that point, was practically nothing, and if no one had done anything about Rowdy, the wail of the sirens out on Concord Avenue might have started him howling.

I knew that Rowdy wasn't the kind of dog you need to approach cautiously.

"Okay," I said emphatically to him. "Okay, big dog."

He stood up, wagged his tail, shook himself, and made a throaty sound somewhere between a sigh and a question. I don't think he knew that Dr. Stanton was dead, but he did know that something strange was happening. I held his collar, unsnapped his leash, disentangled it from the bleacher, and snapped it onto his training collar. He helped by sniffing my ears, nuzzling my neck, and prancing around. I led him over to the others from the eight and eight-thirty classes. By then, he'd decided to adapt to whatever was going on by making himself the center of my attention. He threw me a questioning look, then suddenly flopped belly-up onto the grubby floor, tucked his head in, and curled his forepaws almost under his chin. He was asking me something: "Are you one of the good ones?" I knelt down and massaged his plump white stomach and his massive gray chest.

"You guessed it, buddy," I told him. "When it comes to dogs, I'm a real sap."

People were quiet, and most of the dogs, sensitive to the hushed tones, were subdued. Curly, the irrepressible exception, was pirouetting in front of Diane as if two or three cameras were trained on him. When I stood up, Rowdy reluctantly rolled over and got to his feet. Seeking comfort, nearly everyone had at least one hand on a dog. Ron Coughlin, who'd left the hall with Dr. Stanton, seemed to be the last person who'd seen him alive. Ron was saying that he'd gone to the men's room, and when he'd come out, the entrance hall was empty. He'd assumed that Stanton was outside, as usual.

"Oh, Jesus," Vince said. "There's Roger."

Dr. Stanton's wife had died about twenty years ago. He hadn't had any children. The closest he'd come to a relative was Roger Singer, his nephew, or, more precisely, his great-nephew. Every obedience club has at least one member whom God did not fashion as a dog handler. God did not so fashion Roger. God also makes exceptions to Winter's rule. It would be hard to mold a person more perfectly in the image of Lion, his Newfoundland, than Roger had already been molded, giant-sized and big-boned, with a large head and long black hair. I'd sometimes thought that if you entered Roger in a dog show as a Newfoundland, he'd win Best of Breed.

"I'll get him," said Ray, who'd been replaced at the desk by the Cambridge police. "I'll bet nobody's told him yet."

Ray went back to the desk. By then, the force was there in force, state police as well as Cambridge cops, because the armory is state property. I could see Ray talking with one of the cops at the desk, probably explaining who Roger was, and then I saw him lead Roger and Lion to one of the bleachers. I couldn't hear what they were saying, but Roger kept shaking his head and wiping tears away.

Diane and Lynne were talking about something I'd been thinking about as I was leashing Rowdy.

"It was that thin leather leash, wasn't it?" Diane asked me. Curly always wears a dainty red collar. His leash matches it.

"I didn't see it," I said. I hadn't wanted to look closely. "But it must have been."

Hermes, the Clumber spaniel Lynne had been training that night, was only nine months old. He'd gone to sleep at her feet with his eyes half open. "I asked him about that leash the other night," Lynne said quietly. "It was a new one. I wondered if it was strong enough. I mean, who was I to tell him he was using the wrong lead? But, anyway, I did."

The woman who spoke up next had gray permed curls and wore an Einstein sweatshirt with a Right to Life button pinned to the neckline. Her collie bitch is Princess. I can't remember the woman's name. "It was strong enough after all, wasn't it?" she said.

No one answered her. To anyone who loves dogs, the sensation of holding a leash is the next best thing to the feel of fur. Ever since I was punished at Sunday school for pointing out that "God" spelled backward is "dog," the only religious institution with which I've been affiliated is the American Kennel Club, but I feel the same spiritual comfort holding a leash that others feel holding a rosary. That's how I was raised. In my family, the dog was the sacred animal, like the cow in India. I started to think about how Vinnie's leash had felt when I cleaned it for the last time, and, with that memory, I started to cry, not for Vinnie but for Dr. Stanton and his big, rough dog. Or maybe I was crying for myself, or maybe for all of us. Until that night, this shabby armory had been the safest place in the world, my sanctuary. It certainly was the safest place in Cambridge, the one place where nothing bad could happen. Who'd attack you when you were protected by thirty or forty dogs? And the people were no threat. These were my people, the best people on earth. The armory was the one place in Cambridge where a woman could put down her purse and leave it unguarded. Unless you kept a Yorkshire terrier in your handbag, no one would look twice at it. And now some bastard had spoiled it.

The hardest hit was Barbara, who'd been Dr. Stanton's favorite. If liking frail-looking young women made him sexist, Margaret was right, but Barbara never objected, and when she wants to yell No at a dog, there's nothing frail about her voice. In our regular nine o'clock class, she and Dr. Stanton always trained next to each other. From a distance of more than twenty feet or so, he had trouble seeing Rowdy, and if we left the dogs for sits and downs, she'd keep an eye on Rowdy and let Dr. Stanton know when Rowdy started to move. In return, Dr. Stanton gave her advice she didn't need about Freda and her other German shepherds. Barbara's father died when she was twelve. Afterward, when I told Rita how upset Barbara was about Dr. Stanton, Rita said she had lost her refound object. Rita talks like that. Maybe all therapists do.

Roger, Dr. Stanton's nephew, looked numb and tearful, and lots of us were sad and frightened, but Barbara was the real mourner. She should have gone home, but we weren't allowed to leave. I'm glad she had Freda with her. In looks, Freda is a real contrast to India. She's on the small side for a shepherd, and she's mostly light tan with only a few dark markings on her face and back, but like India, she's amazingly sensitive and intuitive. That night, she melded herself to Barbara's left side, and her big, gentle eyes never left Barbara's face.

We must have hung around for at least an hour. A couple of officers took down our names and addresses. People smoked. The floor is so worn that its finish is completely gone, and in some places, the parquet has crumbled, so Gerry lets people smoke.

"You know what this reminds me of?" Barbara said. "It's weird. It's like a bad dream about a dog show."

She was right. If you're entering one dog in one obedience event, you spend a maximum of maybe fifteen minutes in the ring. Maybe you also exercise the dog once or twice, run through a couple of things with him, and get yourself a cup of coffee. The rest of the time, you hang around. But, of course, that night, there was nothing to watch while we hung around, and when people had to take their dogs out, a cop went along. As Barbara said, it was a nightmare dog show, with no rings set up, no dogs retrieving—or failing to retrieve—dumbbells, and officials striding around who weren't judges and stewards, but cops, including Kevin Dennehy.

"Hey, Holly, how ya doing?" he asked.

If Kevin Dennehy and I both go to Hell and meet in one of its dogless circles, he'll ask how I'm doing. My house is on the corner of Appleton Street and Concord Avenue, not too far from the armory, and his is the first on Appleton Street. Kevin, who's a little older than I am, lives with his mother. She overfeeds him, and he looks as if he isn't fit enough to write out a parking ticket, but he works out at the Y, runs around Fresh Pond every day, and always finishes the Boston Marathon. He has reddish hair and blue eyes. He's possibly the most Irish-looking person in the world. Long before I knew him, he had a dog. The dog died, an event of which Kevin always says, "I could never go through that again." When he says it, he moves his big head back and forth as if I'm holding a puppy out and he's refusing it. I'd always thought of Kevin as a nice guy who needed a dog.

"I'm not doing too well, Kevin," I said.

"Yeah," he said. "Look, you think you could tell me about it?"

"Yeah," I said. "I guess. But I don't know anything."

We moved to the end of the bleachers, near where Rowdy had been tied, and sat down. Rowdy lay down, sniffed the floor, and then kept trying to stick his big nose under the bleachers. Although I've never seen a mouse in the armory, people have told me that there are some and that they live under the bleachers. Maybe Rowdy had found one.

"So what happened?" Kevin asked.

I told him the story, what there was to it.

"This leash," Kevin said when I'd finished. "Wasn't it kind of thin for a husky?"

"Malamute," I said automatically. "People were just talking about it. It was a little thinner than most people would use, but what you use just depends on what you like. The dog doesn't know. Leather's a little more expensive. Dr. Stanton probably paid, oh, I don't know, twelve dollars for that one. Maybe fifteen. He had a lot of money, and dogs were his whole life, so maybe he paid more."

"Did he have any enemies?" Kevin asked.

I had an uncomfortable new take on Kevin. A lot of the time, he was eating too much and running around Fresh Pond and raking leaves from under his barberry hedge, and the rest of the time he was asking whether dead people had had enemies.

"Yes," I said. "But it's a long story. He was an abrasive sort of character. He had a lot of friends, and he had some enemies, but none of them were here tonight."

"What about this guy, uh, Harold Pace?"

"Who?"

"Pace," said Kevin, stroking Rowdy, who had abandoned the mouse game when he discovered that Kevin would pat him. "The guy you saw out there. Big fellow. Blond hair. Collects cans and bottles. You saw him out there."

"Hal," I said. "He's harmless. He ran off. I don't even think Dr. Stanton knew him."

"Look," said Kevin, "I've got to talk to you more. You going to be home tomorrow?"

"Are you telling me not to leave town without informing the police?"

"Right," Kevin said with a grin more subdued than his usual one.

It was not the first time I suspected Kevin of having a slight crush on me. His mother does not have a crush on me. Alcohol is forbidden in her house, and until I bought the house next door to hers, Kevin used to have to sit on the back steps when he wanted a beer, even in midwinter. Kevin is not a heavy drinker. He just likes an occasional Bud when he's been mowing the lawn or shoveling the driveway, and now, if it's cold or rainy, he sometimes sits in my kitchen and sips. Mrs. Dennehy does not approve. Neither does Steve.

"Look, Kevin," I said, "I really don't want to joke around about it. Do you know what happened? Do you have any idea who did this?"

"Well, I'm pretty sure *you* didn't," he said. "Go home. Get out of here. I've got work to do."

A few other people had already been dismissed. The hall was less crowded now, although there remained some trios of cop, handler, and dog in conference. Roger, in one such trio, was leaning against the wall near the open door to the shelter, with Lion, his big Newfoundland bitch, sprawled on the floor at Roger's feet like a gigantic thousand-dollar F.A.O. Schwarz black teddy bear. Ron and Vixen weren't far away, maybe waiting their turn.

Vince and Ray came up to me. Rowdy was tugging and bouncing at the end of the leash and making a persistent throaty growl that was, I hoped, nothing more than his way of pleading with me to take him outdoors. The last time he was out must have been two or three hours ago.

"Holly," Vince said in unusually quiet tones, "I want to talk to you."

"Sure," I said, "but Rowdy's got to go out."

"This won't take a minute," Vince said. "Did they tell you you could leave?"

"Yeah," I said.

"Then why don't you just get your stuff and take Rowdy and go home real quietly. Ray says Roger's got some crazy plan to take Rowdy with him."

"That's not possible." I meant it. I'd have bet anything that whatever provisions Dr. Stanton had made for Rowdy didn't include Roger. It wasn't that Dr. Stanton disliked Roger or anything. I think he just thought that Roger was a big dope. Besides, it hadn't occurred to me that Rowdy would go home with anyone other than me.

"It's not practical," I added. "He can't manage two dogs."

"He can't manage one," Vince said acidly. Vince never, ever said things like that. We were all feeling the strain.

"Just take Rowdy and go," Ray said. "I'll get him tomorrow, or someone will. We'll work it out."

Chapter 3

IF I'm alone, it takes me about ten minutes to walk up Concord Avenue from the armory to my house, which is barn red with three apartments and a fenced yard. I live in the ground-floor apartment, and the rent from the other two apartments pays the mortgage. My friend Rita, the therapist, is on the second floor, and on the third was an assistant professor of English at Harvard who got turned down for tenure because the department found out she drank Cambridge tap water instead of Perrier, didn't listen to National Public Radio, and was once overheard to say "I feel" instead of "One assumes," or at least that was her story.

Of course, what you earn writing about dogs won't pay for a house in Cambridge, even a house in a modest neighborhood at the wrong end of Appleton Street. The Brattle Street end of Appleton Street is posh. It's even more posh than Brattle Street because Brattle Street, for all its mansions, carries plenty of traffic to and from Harvard Square, while Appleton Street is, by Cambridge standards, quiet. Until that night, Dr. Stanton lived on Appleton Street, and not at the humble end. The only reason I could afford a house in Cambridge at all was that Buck had helped me. Even though he thinks I ought to move back to Maine, he was so outraged when I couldn't find an apartment where I could keep a dog that he offered to make a down payment to establish a zone of canine liberation. Naturally, I allow pets in my apartments. Buck feels that the investment in the house is an ethically correct one.

The walk home from the armory took at least twenty minutes that night, maybe more, because Rowdy left his scent on every tree, fire hydrant, lamppost, and hedge on the route. At the corner of Fayerweather, a couple of guys in running gear passed us doing six-minute miles, and Rowdy tried to drag me into dog-team formation after them. At the corner of Walden Street, he spotted an Irish setter taking itself for a walk. His hackles went up, he hit the sidewalk in a flat, ready-to-spring crouch, then he hurled himself forward so hard and fast that I had to bend my knees and brace myself like a martial-arts pro to keep my balance and hang on to his leash. I suppose I should have felt anxious about walking at night along a street where a murderer might be running loose, but Rowdy distracted me. Besides, with him along, I looked protected even though I probably wasn't. Malamutes are the original "Hello, burglar" dogs. They love almost everyone, but at night they look even more like wolves than they do in the daytime.

Whether thanks to Rowdy or not, I arrived home safely. My kitchen is pure, unrenovated 1940s but painted cream with terra-cotta trim to compensate. If you don't look closely, you hardly notice that the cabinets are metal and that what's underfoot is linoleum instead of tile. Rowdy needed water, and I filled a big aluminum saucepan for him. Somehow, I wasn't ready to let him use Vinnie's bowl. He gulped down a quart or so and then started an olfactory survey of the apartment. His hackles went up again, probably at what remained of Vinnie's scent. He checked out the corners and baseboards of the kitchen with special care, then rose on his hind feet, plunked his front paws on the kitchen table, and stuck his big nose into the sugar bowl I'd left out. I yelled No at him, but he'd already licked it clean.

I was half expecting Steve to call or show up. I hadn't seen him since he sent me to phone for the ambulance and the police, but someone had said that he was at the front of the armory, probably in the entrance hall. I figured that he'd know a lot more than I did about what had happened, and it was unlike him not to tell me about it. He has a harder time than you might think when he loses a patient. I thought he'd probably be upset about Dr. Stanton and want to talk about it, but I was hungry and tired, and I wasn't going to wait up for him. I feel a lot for him, but one doesn't want to assume. While I sat at the kitchen table eating a tuna fish sandwich, Rowdy planted himself near me and watched politely. The No had done its work. He was so good that I left a few crusts and put the plate on the floor. One of the many sad things about losing Vinnie was the absence of someone to lick plates and bowls and pans. Every time I had to rinse the egg off a plate, or scrub baked-on cheese off a casserole dish, or lick a bowl myself, I missed her, not that she had much appetite at the end. There's nothing unsanitary about letting a dog prewash the dishes. If you don't mind having your friends eat from your dishes, you shouldn't worry when a dog does.

My bedroom could be pretty, and someday it's going to be. It's painted white and has white shades. The bow window would look great with a window seat, and there's room for a rocking chair and a large dresser. In the meantime, the room is rather sparsely furnished. There's a king-size platform bed with an oak headboard. The comforter, which serves as a bedspread, has little white dots on a navy background. There are drawers under the bed. Vinnie's Orvis dog nest used to be there, too, but I washed the cover and stored her bed in the basement when she died. I am habitually tidy, perhaps because when I was a child, anything I left lying around would end up either chewed or buried.

I decided that Rowdy would be happiest staying in my room. Before I got into bed, I turned off the overhead light and put on my bedside light. The bed has a little built-in nightstand on each side. It's a good bed. I thought it was better to buy one good thing than lots of cheap ones. Rowdy wandered over to me, the tags on his collar jingling. This was no night to be awakened by dog tags. I unbuckled his collar and put it on the nightstand.

I can't explain it, but I think that the moment I undid his collar, he realized that something was wrong. He put both front paws on the bed and stared at me. One thing I like about malamutes is that they're not all supposed to look identical. Rowdy has what's called an open face. His face is all white, with no black around the eyes or on the muzzle, except that his nose is black, the way it's supposed to be. He looked so intelligent that I felt as though I owed him some explanation of what he was doing there. You may think it's stupid, but I gave him one. I also told him about Vinnie.

"She was a real winner," I said. "My mother gave her to me. Now I've lost them both. You have to understand that I'm not looking for a replacement."

He flattened his ears against his head, opened his almond eyes extra wide, and put one great paw in my hand. After I finished talking to him, I turned off the light and slept until seven in the morning, when the phone rang. It was Steve, inviting himself to breakfast. Ordinarily, I'd have told him to go to McDonald's so I could go back to sleep, but I wanted to talk to him before I saw Kevin Dennehy. I wasn't sure what I wanted to tell Kevin about Margaret Robichaud, and Steve could give me some impartial advice. The club fired her more than a year before Steve arrived.

According to the AKC standard, the Alaskan malamute is not a one-man dog, and it was a good thing for Rowdy that he conformed to the standard. He didn't seem to miss Dr. Stanton. I let him into the yard for a minute, and when he came back inside, he followed me to the bathroom door. Vinnie, who loved water, used to stay in the bathroom and keep me company while I showered—she always hoped I'd invite her in—but even when I'd turned the water off and was drying my hair, Rowdy still stood in the hall with a suspicious look on his face.

Steve and India arrived at quarter of eight. I'd told Steve about Rowdy on the phone, and we'd decided that it was okay for him to bring India. Rowdy and India knew one another, and even if they hadn't, a male and female will seldom fight. Two males are another story. And for a deadly slash-and-tear that's all business and no mere ritual bravado, you need two bitches who don't like each other. That may sound like an unfeminist remark, but it's true.

After the dogs sniffed each other and we put them in the yard—I obey the leash law—Steve kissed me. "Good morning, pretty Holly," he said. One of the hazards of talking to dogs a lot is that you start talking to people the same way. He stroked my hair. He has the bluest eyes. "You know, your hair was one of the first things I noticed about you. I wanted to touch it."

"Linatone. Secret of professional groomers. Restores shine and brilliance to the coat. And adds that special zing to scrambled eggs." I put a plate on the table. "So tell me about it," I said as we began to eat.

"I'm not sure I can," Steve said. He's never sure that he can explain anything. In fact, he's used to explaining complicated veterinary matters to worried owners, and he's good at it. He talks quietly and slowly, and he has a warm voice, a good voice for dogs. And women.

"Let me get you started," I said. "You, Lynne, Diane, Ron, and Dr. Stanton were working with Roz. You put the dogs on the long down."

"Right. Lynne and Diane and I went to that corridor behind the desk."

"What time was that?"

"Jesus, I don't know. Quarter of nine? Then you got Diane—Curly got up—and she left. She came back. Then Roz called us all back. I saw you waving at me, and I told you to put the lights on."

"Gerry did," I said.

"Anyway, I knew he was dead the minute I saw him, but I had to do the usual. I told you to get an ambulance."

"And the police," I said.

"Right. It was obvious what had happened. After he took the leash off Rowdy, he put it around his neck. It was that thin leather one, maybe half an inch wide and a quarter inch thick. He and Ron left together, and Ron went to the men's room."

"Why did he do that?" I asked.

"The usual reason, I guess," Steve said. "It does seem kind of strange, but with Vixen, you could leave. With some other dog, you'd know Roz might call you back, but Vixen never gets up. You see Ron as a murderer?"

"Of course not," I said. "It just seemed kind of strange, and I wondered if the police gave him a hard time about it."

"Not that I know of," Steve said. "Next, Stanton went out and stood on the stairs. This is where I'm not sure. Either someone came up to him there, or else someone got him to open the gate and go onto the lawn. In either case, whoever it was got in back of him, reached in front, and grabbed the leash."

"You know, if someone sneaked up on him, he wouldn't necessarily have noticed. I mean, he almost certainly wouldn't have seen anyone, and I'm not sure whether he would've heard. His eyesight was really bad, but I'm not sure how his hearing was."

"Not too good," Steve said, as if he were breaking the news about an aging setter. "Not bad for his age, but not acute, either. He could have been standing on the bottom step. The guy could have left the gate open and waited next to the building, on the lawn. It's dark there. And when Stanton got there, the guy could have gone through the open gate, bending down, and then stood up right behind him. It wouldn't have taken any time. I'll tell you one thing. This guy was no weakling, and he must have done it really fast. I don't think Stanton knew what happened. One second he was standing there, and the next second the leash was so tight he couldn't fight back. He wasn't young, but he was a big man, burly."

"So who was the guy?" I asked.

"This character, what's his name, Pace, I guess. They took him away."

"Oh, shit," I said. "They didn't!"

"Aren't you the one who saw him?"

"Yeah," I said. "I saw him run away, but he always runs away. Or else he comes up and tells you his name, and then he babbles about something. Half the time you can't hear him. Or he'll babble something you can't understand, and then he'll say, 'I'm not supposed to say that.' Obviously, somebody tried to teach him not to say weird things to strangers. But, you know, he just drinks and cashes in his return stuff, and he walks. You see him all over Cambridge. I talk to him sometimes, or at least I try. He likes dogs."

"Then he couldn't possibly have done it, right?"

"It's not that," I said. "I just don't see him as a violent type. You know, if he'd been some ordinary guy in a business suit who happened to be there, they wouldn't have arrested him."

"If he'd been an ordinary guy in a business suit, he wouldn't have been waiting to get into the shelter," Steve said, with some justification, I admit. "But you're right. They would have questioned him, but they probably wouldn't have picked him up. Unless he had some connection with Stanton or something."

"I can't imagine that Hal did," I said. "But, you know, he's a strange-looking guy. Have you ever seen him?"

"Not that I know of."

"If you gave him a bath and shaved him and put him in a Brooks Brothers suit, he'd look as if he were in town for a meeting of the Harvard Board of Overseers or something. He has a purebred look. God, I feel awful. I wish I hadn't said he was there. Speaking of which, I need to ask you about something. You know Margaret Robichaud?"

"By reputation only," Steve said.

"Well, last night, Kevin . . . You remember Kevin the cop?"

"Marathon Man."

I ignored him. "It turns out he's a lieutenant. He showed up and asked some questions, and you may not believe it, but he actually asked if Dr. Stanton had any enemies. It was pretty corny. Anyway, I didn't say anything about the whole mess with Margaret."

"What did you say?"

"Oh, I don't know. That he was abrasive, which is true. Something vague like that. Anyway, Kevin's going to be here today, and, especially with this Hal thing, I think maybe I should just shut up. I mean, I thought she was a god-awful head trainer, and I was glad when she left, but . . ."

"She wasn't there last night, was she?"

"God, no. The club is the last place she'd be."

"Look, why not just tell the truth? You don't have any secret information about her, and the whole thing is public knowledge. If you don't tell him about it, someone else will."

After Steve left to do his Friday morning clinic, I started on my column, an evaluation of electronic flea collars. Vinnie used to sleep at my feet under the kitchen table while I wrote, but Rowdy had apparently decided that the bedroom was his den, and he curled up and slept all morning in the spot where the window seat is going to be. On his afternoon walk, he was less of a monster than I'd expected. An untrained malamute will treat you like a dogsled, but he only dragged me down the street a couple of times, when he saw other dogs. A malamute might not protect you, and he certainly won't protect your house, but if a strange dog ever tries to mug or rob you, you'll be in good paws. By the time we got back from our walk, three people had told me what a nice husky I had. The first time I said he wasn't my dog. The second time I said he was a malamute. The third time I just said "Thanks."

Chapter 4

THE phone was ringing when we got inside, Ray Metcalf asking whether I could meet with him and Lynne and some of the others that night. To my shame, I'd forgotten the matter that was foremost on Ray's mind, not Dr. Stanton's murder but the fun match we'd scheduled for next week. To undo my guilt, I offered to have the meeting at my house, and Ray accepted. As soon as I hung up, I heard Kevin at the door.

"How ya doing, Holly? You're keeping the pooch, huh?"

At the sound of his voice, someone dropped belly-up onto the linoleum, eyes closed in expectant bliss. Not I.

"This is a temporary foster home," I said. "Come in. I've decided to tell you everything."

"Everything. My job's all done, huh?" He stooped over, scratched Rowdy's furry chest, rubbed him under the chin, and said it again in his talking-to-dogs voice. Twice. "My job's all done, huh? My job's all done, huh?"

"No," I said. "I just decided that since you have arrested Hal, who has no motive, you ought to hear about someone who does, at least sort of. That way you can arrest two innocent people instead of only one."

I want to confess at this point that there were two reasons why I thought Hal was innocent. First, he was acting perfectly normal, for him. Second, he reminded me a bit of Buck, except that Buck bathes occasionally and owns a suit he bought at Brooks Brothers about twenty years ago.

I gave Kevin one of the Budweisers he keeps in my refrigerator and told him about the great head-trainer feud.

"The thing started maybe four years ago? Four. Henry McDevitt had been head trainer since forever, and he decided to quit. Retire. He was turning sixty-five. He worked at Polaroid, and he was retiring there and moving to the Cape, Brewster, and he didn't want to do the commute to Cambridge every week, so he resigned. Nobody was happy about it, including me. He was the main reason I joined this club to begin with. I sort of knew him. He's a friend of my father's. Mostly, though, he's just a fantastic trainer."

"So?" Kevin was nursing his beer at the kitchen table, his mind on Budweiser, his right hand around one of Rowdy's paws.

"I'm getting to it. So there was a lot of trouble finding somebody to replace him, naturally, and we ended up with Margaret Robichaud, and don't ask me why. Believe me, it wasn't my decision. The point is, it wasn't Dr. Stanton's idea. They went way back, and, I mean, they could not stand each other, even then. Anyway, Henry was on her side, and I'm sure that didn't hurt. People thought he should have some say in picking his successor. So Dr. Stanton lost round one."

"And he decided to murder her. Wrong way around, Holly."

"Listen. I'm getting to it. Look, Henry was a great trainer. He still is. And Dr. Stanton really was a sort of pillar of the dog world."

Kevin smirked.

"He was," I said. "Don't laugh. But they were both, I don't know, maybe a little less competitive than they used to be. They softened up a bit. But Margaret wasn't beyond it at all. She was like Miss Two Hundred. Miss Perfect." Two hundred is a perfect score in obedience. She was showing all the time, and she actually did have a couple of 200s, which is, how can I explain it? It's a little like Nadia scoring 10.

"Like Bill Rogers in the old days," Kevin suggested.

"Sort of, but everyone likes him. When he was winning the marathon every year, everyone adored him, and now that he doesn't win anymore, everyone still loves him."

"He's a hell of a nice guy."

"Right. That's just what Margaret isn't. She wins, nobody likes her. She loses, nobody likes her. But she doesn't lose a lot, and when the club hired her, she'd been winning big. In obedience. But she'd also been showing in breed, and she'd been doing pretty well there, too. She has goldens."

"Breed?"

"Conformation—to see how the dog matches up to the standard for the breed. His build, coat, color, whatever."

"Like a beauty contest." He kept running an oversize index finger down Rowdy's throat.

"So to speak. So when she applied for the job, people hoped that some of the success would rub off, and in a way it did. I mean, the club got a lot more competitive. Henry was really a good trainer, but compared to Margaret, he's super easygoing, and he was perfect for the people who just want a couple of classes to train the family pet. He's such a nice guy. He's never met a dog he doesn't like. Margaret was just the opposite—she was not interested in the average guy, and she was really not into mixed breeds."

"Mutts?"

"Yeah. And one thing that made it really stupid is that you can get an all-American C.D. with a mixed breed."

"Certificate of deposit?"

"A Companion Dog title. But the main thing is that any dog training club isn't just to teach you to show. It might sound silly, but you're supposed to help make the average dog a good canine citizen. And Margaret used to say all the time, 'We are not here to teach tricks to *pets.*' " She always said "pet" as if it were an obscenity. She was wrong. If "pet" means a good friend, every dog I've ever owned has been a pet. Furthermore, although she bad-mouthed all dogs except goldens, she was an outspoken proponent of the view that all dogs can be trained if you use the right methods, which were, in her view, her methods and her methods only.

"So," I added, "before long, she offended a lot of people. And she didn't really have anything new to say. Jerk on the training collar until the dog does what you want. That was pretty much it. And meanwhile, a lot of us were reading this book by the monks of New Skete."

"Is there any beer left?"

"Yes. You think I'm making this up? I'm not making it up. They live in New York State. Anyway, their idea is that dogs are all descended from wolves, and from the dog's point of view, you're part of his pack. He's part of yours. And one of the things you're doing with a dog is letting him know who's the alpha wolf in the pack. Who's top dog. Because dogs are like wolves. In a way, they *are* wolves. They need to know where they fit, where they belong. And all Margaret was telling us was to jerk harder."

"Does this have something to do with Frank Stanton?"

"Yes. Because he really grabbed onto the book, the whole monks of New Skete thing, and he used all of it against Margaret. It was new ammunition. And anybody who knew anything about wolves or dogs could see what was going on with them, which was a classic leadership struggle to see who was top dog, one alpha against the other. Sometimes they were practically growling at each other. You're the one who asked if he had any enemies."

"He teased her."

"No. He did more than that. He taunted her. He goaded her. Like about the goldens. Goldens really are easy to train, so he'd say, oh, that he'd heard about a nice litter of Akita pups, or he'd tell her about some Irish terrier. He had an Irish terrier himself then. The books always say breeds like that are a challenge. Akitas. Terriers. All the northern breeds: Alaskan malamute, Samoyed, Siberian husky. So the only way for her to shut him up was to get one of the difficult breeds, and she finally took the bait. That was January. It was her second year with the club. She got an Alaskan malamute."

The greatest malamute fans will admit that they're not the easiest dogs to train, and many people will tell you that they're impossible. In other words, in terms of getting one up on Dr. Stanton, she picked a good breed. It was a gutsy thing to do, too, because her chances of ever getting really high scores with a malamute were practically nil. Also, I couldn't imagine anyone less suited to owning a malamute than she was. What she always wanted was a robot, not a dog with a will of its own. Although none of us ever saw her puppy—he was too young to bring to class—we certainly heard about him, and those of us who were reading the monks of New Skete felt a lot of sympathy for him.

"And?" Then he said it to Rowdy. "And?"

"The ploy worked. For a while. Then Dr. Stanton came up with a new route of attack. I guess you could say he turned sneaky. Has anyone told you this already?"

"Just spit it out," he said.

"Okay. He was always a guy who talked a lot. Before that, he didn't exactly gossip, but then he started. I don't think he invented anything. He just passed things along. Rumors."

"Such as?"

"Judging. She's an AKC obedience judge. American Kennel Club. He bad-mouthed her judging. Like he said she favored goldens, which I don't think was true. He said she took points off for right finishes."

"Never. I am shocked."

"Stop fooling with the dog and pay attention, Kevin. The dog is in front of you, and you want him sitting at your left side. In a right finish, he walks past your right side, around in back of you, and sits at your left side. In a left finish, he swings around and ends up sitting at your left side without having walked around you. In the godlike eyes of the AKC, the two finishes are equal. People take this seriously."

"I take it seriously," Kevin said. "She murdered Stanton because his dog walked around him the wrong way."

"Of course not. What I'm telling you is that he got her fired. Or, actually, he just thought he did. He sort of led the anti-Margaret faction, but there really wasn't any pro-Margaret faction. I mean, by the time she left, not one person there thought she was a good head trainer. All she did was criticize everyone. And the membership was really dropping off." Each beginners' class would start out with the usual twenty or thirty newcomers, and all but four or five would be gone by the third lesson. "So it probably wasn't a big surprise to her when she was actually fired, but it was worse than it had to be. Dr. Stanton won the battle, so you'd think he might have been gracious about it, but for one thing, his dog had just died, and, believe me, he was not in a charitable mood. And he never softened up, even after she was gone. A couple of months after she left, we heard that her malamute had died, and Dr. Stanton kept hinting that it was no accident." No one believed him. In fact, no one paid any attention. By then, we were caught up in Vince's enthusiasm. His belief in the power of praise was contagious. We'd all started to praise one another again, too, and we wanted to forget about Margaret.

"So did she kill the dog or what?" Kevin asked.

"I don't think so," I said. "I heard it ran off. A malamute on the loose can really go places. It probably got hit by a car. I don't know. End of story. I can tell you were enthralled. So tell me about Hal."

"Harold Pace," Kevin said. "A juicer. In and out of Met State."

"Met State." Cambridge is a weird place. If a Harvard professor thinks he's God, that's normal, but if he announces it too often in public, he goes to McLean Hospital. Met State is where Harvard professors don't have to go.

"And then the liberals came along and discovered deinstitutionalization." It's hard to tell which word Kevin says with more scorn, *liberal* or *deinstitutionalization.*

"I figured he'd been hospitalized off and on," I said. "But what does he have to say? Do you seriously think he had something to do with it?"

"We're going to hold him till he dries out, but in my opinion, he has no notion of what he did—or of anything else, either."

"But what would make him do it? Why would he want Dr. Stanton dead?"

"You tell me," Kevin said. "He won't."

If I'd been smarter, I'd have got Kevin to tell me about Hal first thing, and then maybe I wouldn't have told him about Margaret—but it didn't matter, I thought. Kevin probably knew that I was about to spill something, and he'd probably decided not to tell me anything until I spilled it. I was glad I'd disappointed him. In any case, I decided, no one commits murder because she's been fired by a dog training club. Margaret's only crime was a gift for putting people off. Besides, the armory was the last place she'd have been, the scene of her big failure, and, as Steve had pointed out, someone was bound to tell the police about her anyway.

By the time Kevin left, I'd lost my energy for electronic flea collars, and Rowdy was prowling around looking hopeful, so I took him for a short walk. On Donnell Street, he spotted a black cocker spaniel moored to a clothesline trolley. The cocker yapped and lunged, and Rowdy, hackles up, let loose a harsh rumble from deep in his chest. He lunged, too, but I caught my balance in time and managed to stay upright. Otherwise, he was pretty good. When we got home, I still wasn't in the mood for flea collars, and since Rowdy was full of energy, we did a little work.

If you've never trained a dog, you may think that Rowdy was learning to roll over or give his paw. An obedience-trained dog will learn the tricks easily, but they're not what training is about. Curly, Diane's miniature poodle, can dance on his hind legs and jump into her arms, but to get his first title, his C.D., which he'll probably do any day now, he won't do any tricks. If he tries any in the ring, as he's done before, he'll lose points. He'll heel on and off leash. Sit. Stand and stay in the same place. Come when he's called. Do a long sit for one minute and a long down for three.

Unspectacular? Yes. And a million times harder than saying his prayers or playing dead. Vinnie was the best obedience dog I'll ever own. As I knew even before I heeled Rowdy up and down my block of Appleton Street that day, he was no Vinnie. His idea of heeling was forging ahead, which means walking out in front, taking *me* for a walk. And speaking of being in the lead, he more than hinted that he was the alpha wolf in our little pack. He nipped at the leash, a lot closer to my hands than I liked. Malamutes have large, sharp teeth. One of his cute tricks was to nip at the leash at exactly the same time he was doing precisely what he was supposed to be doing. That way, if I rewarded the good behavior, I also rewarded the nipping, and if I corrected one, I corrected the other.

In between the forging ahead and the nipping and a few other alpha-wolf tactics, he also showed me that he was a dog who worked with joy. When I told him to heel—he'd been taught to finish right—he'd first bounce in the air, then leap around me, and then bounce again into his sit. You can teach a dog to quit the theatrics, but if he doesn't have any zip to begin with, he never will.

Chapter 5

"POOR baby," Barbara Doyle cooed as she ran her tiny manicured right hand over Rowdy's head and down the soft white fur on his throat. Barbara stands no more than five feet tall. Someone who didn't know Winter's rule would interpret her fluffy hair and frilly blouses as a sign that she owned one spoiled Pekinese, but if Barbara's three German shepherds ever decide to register her, the official name they choose will be Velvet Glove's Iron Fist.

Eight of us had finished eating two large pizzas. We sat in my living room, which is painted white. It has a fireplace and one large couch. The fireplace works. When I visit Buck, I usually bring back a load of firewood. I'd made a fire that night. Barbara and Vince were sharing the couch with Ray and Lynne Metcalf. Roz, Ron, Arlene, and I were on the floor by the fireplace. Arlene is a heavy, nondescript person with two greyhounds that look like Ray and Lynne Metcalf. Cambridge has more greyhounds per person than any other place I've ever been. Almost all of them are retired racing dogs rescued from death. They make sweet, gentle pets. Life as a racing greyhound is really hellish, so their adoptive homes must seem like paradise.

Curling up on a warm hearth or next to a radiator is a sign of illness in northern breeds, so Rowdy was avoiding us. He'd displayed unexpectedly good manners while we were eating. I'd offered to put him out until we finished the pizza, but we decided to give him a chance to behave, and he hadn't tried to steal a thing. When we were done with the pizza, Vince, who knows better, made an experimental toss with a piece of crust, and Rowdy leapt up and caught it. His jaws closed with the sound of a trap snapping shut.

"I know I told you someone would get him today." Ray sounded guilty.

"He's been fine," I said.

"The fact is . . ." Ray started to say.

"The fact is," Lynne continued, "that we're expecting, and we aren't going to have room."

The Metcalfs are beyond childbearing age. The Clumber spaniels are not. It was obvious that Ray had suggested to Lynne that they offer Rowdy temporary kennel space, and she'd refused.

"Maybe Millie would like him," Barbara said.

Frank Stanton kept a library of dog books that he shared with our club and several others, so everyone knew his housekeeper, Millie Ferguson, who was even tinier than Barbara Doyle and at least five years older than Dr. Stanton.

"I don't think she has the strength to handle him," I said. "She can't manage the heavy work anymore. Has Roger lost interest?"

I would never, of course, have turned Rowdy over to that big dope, but the club was still reacting against Margaret Robichaud's negativism, and I didn't want to sound like her. I needn't have worried. Dr. Stanton had observed Roger training Lion, although *training* is hardly the right word.

"Frank and I had a talk about it last spring," Ron said. In addition to being a plumber and the owner of Vixen, Ron is our treasurer. He has a round, ruddy face, and the hair he has left is blondish. "We arranged a sort of deal. I told him that if anything happened, we'd find a home for Rowdy. In return, we get his books."

"Where are we supposed to put them?" Arlene asked.

"Won't Roger let us leave them where they are?" Barbara asked. "It isn't as though people go there all that often."

"Something tells me we aren't going to be seeing too much of Roger from now on," Arlene said. She seldom worries about the impression she's making. "Hasn't the possibility crossed your mind that his interest in obedience might have some remote connection with his interest in a certain inheritance?"

"But he really loves Lion," I objected. How could he not? Newfoundlands are sweet dogs, and Lion was outstandingly sweet even for a Newfie.

"Of course he loves Lion," Arlene said. "But if you ask me, that was an accident. If you want my opinion, the reason he got a dog in the first place was to ingratiate himself with Frank. Just watch. He'll take the money and run."

"And we'll have a roomful of books and no place to put them," said Roz.

"I'm not even a hundred percent sure we're getting them," Ron said. He's usually an up-front guy, but his face had an odd, shifty expression. "Mostly, he wanted to make some plans for Rowdy, and after all he's done, what could I say?"

In addition to working for the club and letting us use the library, Dr. Stanton always donated the trophies for our big annual obedience trial as well as the trophies for the highest-scoring dog in each class at our little fun matches. The primary purpose of a fun match like the one we'd scheduled for the following Thursday is exactly what the name suggests: fun. It also gives the dogs and handlers a chance to practice in the ring. Any dog, including a mixed breed, is welcome. The only thing the winners expect is a ribbon or, if the dogs are lucky, a ribbon plus a few dog biscuits. Trophies aren't necessary, but they add a special touch to our fun matches.

"You could have consulted with us," Roz said to Ron. "A full-grown malamute isn't all that easy to give away if you're fussy about a good home."

"You know how much Frank donated last year?" said Ron. "Was I supposed to tell him thanks, we really appreciate everything, and as soon as you're buried, we'll drive Rowdy to Angell?"

Angell Memorial is a big veterinary hospital with what's optimistically called an adoption ward.

"Of course not," Roz said. "But you might have let us know."

"Okay, I probably should've let you know," Ron conceded, "but I didn't expect him to die. Did you?"

"Look," said Vince, who's used to stepping calmly into the midst of snarling, "could I remind everyone that we've got business to take care of? Let's worry about the books if and when we get them. For now, they can stay where they are. Roger isn't going to burn them. The dog is our real responsibility. Obviously, Frank realized that Roger couldn't provide an appropriate home for him."

"All right! I get the message," I said. "I now own a future Utility malamute."

Everyone laughed. Utility Dog is the third of the three obedience titles, and it's easier to shove a camel through the eye of a needle than it is to put U.D. on a dog. If you intend to try, you start with a golden retriever, a German shepherd, a Rottweiler, a poodle, a corgi . . . just about anything but a malamute. Getting a malamute for obedience purposes is not very rational. In fact, as I demonstrated that night, the main reason you get a malamute is that you're not rational on the subject of dogs.

"Congratulations," Lynne said. "We knew it wouldn't be too difficult to pull this off."

If I'd been with a group of malamute breeders and had just decided to take some abandoned runt, all of them, somewhere in their hearts, would have felt a secret glee that my dog would never defeat theirs in breed, what Kevin had called the beauty contest. Obedience isn't like that, especially at my club. Obedience competition is God's way of making a point about humility. Anytime you start to feel too superior to another handler, God (Remember? "Dog" spelled backward) intervenes by inspiring your dog to wander around the ring or to lift his leg on one of the hurdles.

"Look," Vince said, "we've got a match scheduled for Thursday night. I would like to know what your feelings are about it. Do we cancel?"

"Dr. Stanton would have hated that," I said.

"We don't have any choice," Arlene said. "Nobody wants to think about it, but the fact is, the same thing could happen again. Are we going to have people show up when there's some lunatic loose?"

"In the first place, the police arrested someone," Roz said. "And in the second place, no one's going to stand outside alone."

"They don't know the guy did it," I said. "One of my neighbors is a cop. They're just holding him. They don't have any proof."

"So it's not safe," Arlene said. "I mean, the shelter's still open. Anybody could come along. One of those people may have something against dogs."

I did not point out that someone with something against dogs would have strangled a borzoi or a dachshund, not an ophthalmologist.

"We don't know that someone from the shelter did it," Lynne said. "It could have been anyone."

"Not really," Ray said.

"So do we cancel?" Vince is what some Cambridge types call task-oriented.

"There must be something we can do," Lynne said. "If we cancel, you know, we really cancel. We can't postpone it a week or two. The judges have been lined up for months. I don't think everyone realizes how much work goes into this."

"The real point is," Ron said, "that Holly's right. Canceling the match is the last thing Frank would have wanted."

"He was looking forward to it," Arlene admitted.

"More than that, he was going to enter," Roz said. "You know, one of the reasons he quit going to shows was his eyesight. He was afraid he'd bump into things and stuff. And besides, Rowdy wasn't ready. But he thought that since all of us knew about his sight, and since we'd all seen what Rowdy was like when Frank first started with him, it would be nice to give it a try, Novice or maybe Pre-Novice."

When Dr. Stanton first started with Rowdy, the big mal

had dragged him through every training session, challenged all the other dogs, and convinced every member of the Cambridge Dog Training Club that malamute vocalizations are designed to carry leagues across the tundra. Any trainer except Vince would have kicked Rowdy out of the class.

"Novice," Arlene said. "Some of those people in Pre-Novice won't have had more than four or five lessons. He thought it'd be unfair to them."

"I have a thought about security," Barbara said quietly. "I think it would be possible to organize a patrol. That way, if safety is the real issue, we wouldn't have to cancel."

She volunteered her three German shepherds, with herself and her husband to handle two of them. Ron agreed to handle the third. Vince offered his cousins, Tony and Alice, with their two Rottweilers, and the Metcalfs promised to line up a few more people and dogs. Pending Steve's approval, I donated him and India, and I said I'd talk to Kevin.

"Hey, I've got a great idea," Barbara said to me as everyone was leaving. "You can enter Rowdy! Really, what we can do is have the whole thing be a sort of tribute, and there's nothing he would have loved better than having Rowdy there."

Forging ahead and nipping at my hands.

"Barbara," I said, "that's a lovely idea, but he's not ready."

"So enter him in Pre-Novice," Lynne said.

Official trials don't even have a Pre-Novice or Sub-Novice class, which means just what it sounds like: rank beginner. Buck and Marissa raised me to be a good sport.

"He's too advanced," I said. "It wouldn't be fair."

"So put him in Novice, like Frank would have wanted. It's just a fun match," Arlene said. "We know what he's like."

She was right. I was suffering from pride. There is nothing that makes the human face burn like having a dog embarrass you in the ring. The ring is the only place I ever blush. Lots of people have dreams about walking down the street and suddenly realizing that they don't have any clothes on. I have nightmares about walking around the ring and suddenly finding that I don't have any dog at heel.

"I'll think about it," I said.

"I'm entering you in Novice," said Vince. Vince, I thought, must be one of those rare people born with an immunity to ring blush. "See you at the funeral, I guess."

When they were gone and I was tidying up, I found a navy-blue jacket that someone had left on one of the kitchen chairs. It's not polite to go through people's pockets, but I didn't know whose jacket it was, and there might be ID in it. In the left pocket of the jacket was a plastic bottle from Huron Drug. According to the label, the pills in the bottle were Valium prescribed for Vincent Dragone. The secret of his imperturbability? Twenty minutes later, he called to ask whether he'd left his jacket.

"Oh, it's yours," I said with what I hoped was a tone of surprise. "I wondered whose it was."

He stopped by to pick it up, then I went to bed. I had bad dreams. "See you at the funeral," Vince kept telling me. Books sometimes tell you that it's good for children to have pets because the inevitability of losing a pet helps teach children to come to terms with death. Compared to human beings, dogs have a short life span, so with all of the dogs in my family, the real inevitability was that I had too many lessons too early. I sometimes concoct private last rites of my own, but I will do anything to avoid even the possibility that I might have to go to a real funeral.

On Saturday morning, after I called Kevin and extracted a promise of official help with security for the match, I set out for Maine. My new dog had so much scrap and hustle that with less fur and more height, he'd have been a Red Auerbach pick for the Celtics' starting five. I was taking him to training camp.

Chapter 6

THE drive to Owls Head takes about four hours if you don't stop, but we took a break on the Maine Turnpike at what claimed to be a restaurant. It sold what it claimed was coffee. I took the paper cup out to the Bronco. After one taste, I threw the cup into a trash barrel, got out the thermos of water, and filled its cup for me and a stainless-steel bowl for Rowdy. The thermos and bowl were the ones I always used to take to shows. Some of us are careful about the water available at shows. A change in water can upset a dog's digestion. An accident in the ring is humiliating for a dignified dog, and it means automatic disqualification.

We hit Owls Head at about two. When Marissa was alive, the house looked like an illustration for a *Down East Magazine* article on coastal perennial gardens. It's on a narrow, pine-lined blacktop road that tourists mistake for the real Maine. The real Maine is dirt roads that lead to tar-paper shacks. It's cellar homes with no houses on top. Buck is trying hard to restore reality to Owls Head. He has a way to go. Patches of white paint remain on the wood shingles. Marissa's peonies and day lilies still bloom in the summer, but most of the garden space now belongs to turnips for the deer, sunflower and thistle for the birds. A double row of pines now blocks the view of the house from the road. The tourists who used to slow down to admire the garden can barely see the house. If they catch a glimpse and hear the howling, they must assume that behind the trees lives one of those famous Down East backwoods characters they've read about in vanity-press publications sold at souvenir shops. Although Down East doesn't begin until Ellsworth, and little Owls Head is backwoodsy only by contrast with Old Orchard Beach, they won't entirely have missed the point. Buck knows more about dogs than any other living human being, and if that makes someone a character, a character he is.

I parked the Bronco in front of the once-red barn. The wolf dogs do not run free, but I thought Rowdy might cause chaos if he started poking his nose into their kennels, so I leashed him. Buck, who must have heard the car and the howling and barking and who has a sixth sense for the presence of a new dog on his turf anyway, emerged from the kitchen door. Fifty-five, six one, with thick Yankee features, he's a graying, blue-eyed moose dressed in wolf-shredded L.L. Bean, a looming, shabby presence.

"Well, hello, big fellow," he said. If moose could speak, they'd have Buck's deep, smooth voice. "Aren't you a beauty! What does she call you?" His eyes glitter when he talks to dogs. In his half-wild way, he's a handsome man.

Rowdy, who knew even then not to jump on people, rose on his hind legs, wagged his plumy tail, rested his forepaws on Buck's chest, and tried to lick his face. Malamutes have large tongues.

"Rowdy," I said. "Hello, Dad."

"Where'd Rowdy come from?" Buck was obviously pleased. He's easy to please. All you have to do is get a dog.

"Frank Stanton via the Cambridge Dog Training Club. You heard?"

"Heard it through the grapevine. Rowdy of Nome, huh?"

"Rowdy of Cambridge," I said.

"Rowdy of Nome was one of the first malamutes in the stud book," Buck said. He loves to pontificate. "Nineteen thirty-five. The original Kotzebue line. That's what this dog is. A big Kotzebue."

I now know that a Kotzebue dog is descended from the ones bred in the thirties at the Chinook Kennels in New

Hampshire, the original dogs registered when the AKC first recognized the Alaskan malamute. I know lots of other facts about the history of Alaskan malamutes, too. Buck's wolf dogs are part malamute.

We stood out in the cold while he lectured. He cannot abide ignorance about dogs, and he was dressed for coastal Maine in November. The high point of his story was the low point in malamute history. Shortly after World War II, at the end of an Antarctic expedition, the commander of a naval vessel that was supposed to transport the dogs home put all of the expedition's malamutes on an ice floe, set a time bomb, and left, thus destroying most of the foundation stock of a breed already depleted after service in the war. I didn't want to hear any more, and when Buck started on the great debate about whether there was any wolf in the original malamutes, I seized the opportunity.

"Speaking of wolves," I said, "aren't introductions overdue?"

When I say that Buck shares his house with the wolf dogs, I don't mean that all of them live in the house all the time. They follow a fixed rotation schedule. Each one gets to be a house dog about once every two weeks, except that Buck makes frequent exceptions for Clyde, who is really his pet. The others are kennel dogs. Don't feel sorry for them. The kennels are large chain link runs with concrete floors, and each run leads to a stall in the barn. Many people, including Buck, live in houses that are less meticulously clean than those kennels and stalls.

It just happened to be Clyde's turn as house dog. Buck brought him out, but we kept both dogs on leash for the first few minutes. Rowdy bounded around, sniffed, and otherwise lived up to his name. Clyde, who looks like a lean, leggy, timid malamute, stood stiffly and did his best to ignore Rowdy. We unleashed them both and stood back. Rowdy moved in close. Clyde turned slowly so that his left side faced Rowdy. Rowdy tried to sniff his rear end. Clyde lifted one upper lip in an Elvis Presley sneer, displayed a set of teeth about twice the size of Rowdy's, and emitted a single low growl. Rowdy got the message. He assumed the universal doggy let's-play pose—rump up, forelegs bent, shoulders down—and Clyde mirrored him. I watched their rough-and-tumble for a minute, then went in out of the cold.

The inside of my parents' house still looks more or less the way it did when I was growing up except that Marissa used to hire someone to clean. Now, if you comment on the fur, Buck asks with alarmed concern in his voice, "You're not allergic, are you?" His nasal passages have adapted so completely to dander that he would probably sneeze and cough if fate forced him into an enclosed space that had never known the presence of a dog. He breathes with particular ease in the kitchen.

I've always loved that kitchen. The sink is real slate, not soapstone. The stove is a Modern Glenwood Wood Parlor. There's a brick fireplace, and the floor is brick-red tile that my mother laid herself when tile was only practical, not fashionable. The curtains ought to be replaced. They're red. It took me a long time to understand that red is supposed to signal danger. For me, it always meant safety because it's what you wear in deer season if you don't want to get shot.

Buck and Rowdy came in. Clyde was in his kennel. Asking him for hospitality might have been pushing it. Buck filled a large tarnished sterling-silver engraved bowl with water and put it on the floor by the sink. Marissa, whose dog won that bowl, always polished it. She kept it, filled with fruit, on the sideboard in the dining room, surrounded by other trophies. Buck never polishes the trophies, and the ones he uses for the dogs have a few dents.

With a cup of that disgusting instant coffee he likes, Buck joined me at the table.

"So let's see his papers," he said with a smile.

"I don't have them," I said.

"I'm glad your mother isn't here," he said sternly. He wasn't joking. "She'd be very disappointed in you, Holly."

"I'm getting them. I just don't have them yet," I said.

* * *

If you ever need to get a dog in shape fast, go to Buck's. On Sunday morning, he cajoled Rowdy into hopping onto his new toy, a giant electronic scale (no lifting), and verified my impression that my new dog was not just big, but overweight. We started on a program of exercise, a five-mile walk each morning and again each afternoon, with two training sessions a day as well. In between, Rowdy played with Clyde and slept. The solution to the nipping problem was Buck's suggestion, a nylon training collar in place of the chain one. On Buck's advice, I also did something that would have shocked Marissa. I used food to reward Rowdy for the recall. It worked. By Wednesday, although he still forged ahead and still didn't look at me when he was heeling, his work wasn't too bad. The only preparation left was to bathe and groom him.

Most people don't bother to bathe a dog for a fun match. In fact, even for a real obedience trial, it isn't necessary, since he's judged on behavior, not looks, but I think that it creates a sloppy impression to walk into the ring with an ungroomed dog. Also, in case the dog hasn't guessed already, it doesn't do any harm to let him know that a special occasion is coming up.

When I bathe my dogs in Cambridge, I have to use my own bathtub, which means that if I'm not careful the next time I bathe and groom myself, I end up washing my hair with Hills Flea Stop and conditioning it with Ring 5 Coat Gloss.

At Buck's, bathing should have been easy because Marissa built a dog spa in the barn. It's a little heated room with a sunken concrete tub so the dog doesn't have to climb over anything to get in. She installed a powerful spray that lets you rinse thoroughly. There's a big pile of thick towels, a blow dryer on a long cord, a grooming table, and a set of grooming equipment—brushes, combs, nail trimmers. Rowdy took one look and backed up. When I unbuckled his leather collar, slipped on the training collar and leash, and tried to lead him to the tub, he braced his front paws and growled in much the way Clyde had growled at him. I thought I knew the solution. I let go of his leash, took off my shoes and socks, rolled up my jeans, stepped into the tub, and splashed around. I told him what a lovely time I was having. I pointed out that he was missing out on the fun. The ploy failed. He went to the door and raked it with his claws.

Hanging on a hook on the wall was a modern muzzle that Buck must have bought or been given, because they didn't make this kind when Marissa was alive. It's made of soft webbing, and it fastens with Velcro. I clamped it on Rowdy, picked up his leash, pulled him toward the tub, wrapped my arms around his hindquarters, and pushed him in. I'm stronger than I look. It occurred to me that Dr. Stanton must have stuck to dry baths.

Fifteen minutes later, the blow dryer was running, I was brushing, and Rowdy, sprawled on a bed of towels on the floor, was nearly comatose with bliss. I was using a soft brush on his underbelly and inner thighs when I found the tattoo, smaller and much closer to the hock of his hind leg than tattoos usually are.

A tattoo on a dog isn't, of course, a heart with "Mother" inside. It's an identification number, usually the owner's Social Security number or the dog's AKC registration number, tattooed either inside an ear or on the inner thigh. This one read WF818769, obviously not a Social Security number. I wasn't surprised to find that he'd been tattooed. Dr. Stanton was careful. My only surprise was that I hadn't noticed it before. This was the first bath I'd given Rowdy, but I'd brushed him a couple of times. Apparently, the idea of locating the tattoo near the hock and making it small had been to keep it almost invisible unless you were looking for it. It seemed to me that hiding the tattoo defeated one of its main purposes—to get back a lost dog—but the cosmetic result was perfect.

* * *

We left for Cambridge early Thursday afternoon, but, thanks to a minor breakdown on the turnpike that cost us a couple of hours, we arrived late for the match, with no time to go home. All of the outside floods were on at the armory, and the patrols were visible. Steve and India were walking back and forth near the entrance. India's wide-open eyes were fastened on Steve. She always looks as if she's asking whether there's some service she can render him.

"We just got in," I said, and explained about the breakdown. I'd called Steve on Saturday to let him know where I was. "I'm sorry I copped out on the work."

"No problem," he said, and patting Rowdy, added, "You're doing your share."

"This dog isn't work," I said. "He's therapy."

I meant it. I hadn't felt so happy since before Vinnie died. Because I had a dog again, life was okay. I was sorry Dr. Stanton was dead, but the truth is that if bringing him back to life had meant returning Rowdy, I might not have done it even if I'd had the choice. As I've said, I'm not rational when it comes to dogs.

Our spring fun match is a big deal locally. We list it in *The Match Show Bulletin,* and people come from all over the place. The fall one is just for the club. Two rings were going when Rowdy and I walked in: Novice and Open. Pre-Novice must have been earlier, and we never have enough people to do Utility at the fall match. In the ring closer to the door, Diane and Curly were doing Open. When Curly feels like it, he heels off leash so perfectly that you'd swear there's an invisible lead running up from his little red collar to Diane's hand. That's how he was heeling when I walked in. Afterward, Diane would probably say that he'd known it was only a fun match. In the back ring, a skinny guy with a big mixed breed named Caesar was doing Novice. Caesar was lagging. A bigger crowd than I'd expected was standing around watching. I was glad to know that we weren't people who scared easily.

Arlene was at the desk. Her hair looked oily. She needs

to lose thirty or forty pounds. She could have used Rowdy's rehab program. But her looks don't bother her.

"I thought you weren't going to make it," she said. "You're next, and you're the last dog. Vince signed you up. Doesn't he look gorgeous?"

She meant Rowdy, not Vince.

"He's really a sweetheart," I said. "Novice?"

She nodded. "Let them know you're here."

I put my stuff—my purse, an extra leash, Rowdy's regular leather collar, the thermos, the bowl—on one of the bleachers at the far end of the hall and tossed my jacket on top. In the Novice ring, Caesar was finishing the recall, his last individual exercise. He came in crooked. I put on my armband, and the steward, a guy from beginners' who has a basset, spotted me.

I said a few words to Rowdy before I led him into the ring. "It's okay if you forget. Just do your best," I whispered.

The judge, a brown-haired, fortyish woman in a peach polyester suit, was one I hadn't met before.

"Are you ready?" she asked. She wasn't curious. It's a required question.

"Ready," I said.

On leash, he forged a little, I thought, except on the outside turn of the figure eight, where I had the feeling he was lagging. (Since good handling means looking at the judge and looking where you're going, you don't always see what your dog's doing.) Off leash, his sits seemed a little slow. His stand for examination was perfect, but it's a pretty easy exercise. Recall isn't, but he was close to perfect anyway, and when he finished, he bounced to a sit and smiled up at me. I released him and gave him a hug. Praise is allowed in the ring between exercises.

After a break of only a couple of minutes, we were called back for the group exercises, the long sit and long down. He'd done them so well all week that I should have been suspicious. Since this was Novice, not Open, we stayed in the ring when we left the dogs. On the long sit, Rowdy squirmed, which would lose us points. On the long down, I thought for sure he was going to try to crawl over to Lion, who was next to him, but he caught my eye and held still.

We all left the ring to wait. There were a couple of handlers and dogs still waiting for Open, and then there'd be the group exercises for Open. After that, the judges would finish adding up the scores and would check their arithmetic. Finally, everyone who'd qualified would be called back for the ribbons and trophies. I didn't know what our score would be, but I was sure we'd qualified.

I'd missed dinner in order to get to the match, and I was hungry and thirsty. Rowdy probably was, too. There was a bottle of water in the car, but I'd discovered in Maine that Rowdy was one of those dogs who'd eat or drink anything—salad, grapes, bananas, peanuts, popcorn, tomato juice, orange juice—so I dug under my jacket, pulled out the thermos and bowl, and poured both of us some orange juice, which was what I'd filled it with at Buck's. The orange juice tasted kind of funny to me, but I was so thirsty that I drank it anyway. After the drive to Owls Head, I'd left the thermos sitting in the Bronco all week, so I figured that it must have got moldy and that I hadn't washed it well enough before I put in the orange juice that morning. Or maybe I'd used the wrong pitcher and got some of Buck's Tang or Gatorade by mistake, or, just possibly, some orange-flavored nutritional supplement for lactating bitches, but it didn't worry me. Buck believes you shouldn't feed a dog anything you wouldn't eat or drink yourself, and vice versa. Rowdy didn't seem to notice the taste, but my deity looks after her own. If that judge had taken another few seconds to tally up the scores, I'd have refilled Rowdy's bowl.

As it was, we were called to the ring before I had a chance. The Pre-Novice trophy went to a golden handled by Rick Lawson. No one was surprised. As I'd predicted, Curly won Open. We won Novice. Steve and India were second, only because she'd messed up the recall by wandering around before she got to Steve. The sleepiness hit me while people were crowding around patting Rowdy and telling me how happy Dr. Stanton would have been. That was true. I remember nearly starting to cry, then yawning, then thinking what a long drive I'd had. The next thing I recall was some disconnected memories of what turned out to be the Mt. Auburn Hospital.

The hospital room was too sunny the next morning. The light kept hurting my eyes while Steve was telling me that Rowdy and I had been overdosed with Valium. Sometime later in the morning, someone told me that Steve rushed Rowdy to his clinic as soon as he had told Ray to take me to Mt. Auburn. Steve has his priorities straight.

Chapter 7

By Saturday morning I was healthy enough and ripping mad. Some bastard had overdosed my dog before he was even officially my dog. At eleven I checked out of Mt. Auburn and walked the four or five blocks home. I walked a little shakily, but I walked. The Bronco (Steve had saved it from towing) was parked in the driveway behind my house, my suitcase still in the back.

Steve used his lunch break to drop off Rowdy, who seemed to have shed a few pounds, and as soon as Steve left, Kevin knocked on the back door. He was carrying a paper grocery bag and wanted to make himself a hamburger. For reasons unknown to me, Mrs. Dennehy had left the Roman Catholic Church to become a Seventh-Day Adventist. Kevin isn't allowed to keep, cook, or eat meat in her house.

Kevin can't cook, but he knows better than to ask me to do it, so we talked over the sound and smoke of ground beef burning in a cast-iron frying pan.

"What are your thoughts on Ronald Coughlin?" he asked, poking ineffectually at the pan.

"My thoughts are that he has one of the best-trained dogs I've ever seen," I said. "If he hadn't been patrolling on Thursday night, he might have won Open. And he's a terrific plumber."

"We're interested in his visit to the can," Kevin said.

"I thought you were interested in Hal Pace."

"Still don't know what the deal is with him, but he's out of the last one."

"How did that happen?"

"No access. You carried that thermos into the armory, dumped your stuff on the bleachers, and left it. Pace wasn't in the building. As a matter of fact, he was soaking up the air at Leverett House. There was some kind of a problem."

Harvard kids live in houses, not dormitories. That makes it easier to pretend that this is Cambridge, England, instead of the gauche New World. Outside Leverett House are some big vents where the university expels excess heat, and on cold nights, homeless people gather around to get warm. Since their presence doesn't add any Old World charm, the university keeps trying to screen off the vents and drive the people away. I knew what the problem was because I'd read the *Globe* while I was in the hospital. Some of the kids had organized a demonstration to protect the rights of the homeless to Harvard's stale heat. Hal must have been seen there.

"Coughlin," Kevin said. He'd scraped the meat onto two cold hamburger rolls, one generously intended for me, and he'd added ketchup, which was dripping down his blond-furred wrists.

"Ever the loyal Republican," I said.

"What?"

"According to Reagan, it's a vegetable. Ketchup."

"Damn straight," Kevin said. "Talk about Coughlin."

"Ron Coughlin is the treasurer of the club. He's a nice guy."

"Access to funds," Kevin said.

"There are no funds. We charge a few dollars a lesson. From that, we pay rent to the armory, and we pay Vince and Roz about a tenth of what they're worth. We pay insurance. We did two matches and one show last year, and we couldn't have done those without help."

"From Stanton."

"He donated trophies, and I think he gave something, too. Did you think that Ron was absconding with the club treasury? Have you called a plumber lately? The club could run for a year on what he charges to install a bathroom sink. Besides, treasurer is the worst job there is. It's all paperwork, and the fact that there's never enough money doesn't help."

"Right," Kevin said, and, pointing to the second hamburger sitting in its pool of congealed grease, added, "You don't want this? Still under the weather?"

"Not quite myself yet," I lied. "But thanks. You have it."

"You see, Holly," he said, "in my opinion, some of these people are fanatical. Not you, but some of these people. And this Coughlin strikes me as one of them. Now, here he is, adding up this nickel-and-dime stuff. All his buddies are hoping Stanton will come through again. And all the time, Coughlin knows something the rest of you don't know: that once the old boy's offed it, it's all yours."

"I don't know what you're talking about," I said.

"The housekeeper gets a little something. The nephew does, too. A couple of other dog outfits get a little something. You people get the rest," Kevin said. "One dog. One house. With contents. Plus the rest. Six or eight hundred thousand dollars, they aren't sure yet."

"You're joking." I wondered whether the rest of the club knew yet. And, uncharitably, I wondered whether Roger Singer knew.

"When I heard it, I almost fell off the chair," he said. "Left it to a bunch of dogs. If you're a fanatic, that's a motive. I haven't got it worked out yet, but you know that's got to be one piece of it."

As soon as Kevin left, I called Ron Coughlin, not, of course, to ask whether he'd strangled Dr. Stanton or overdosed Rowdy and me, but to ask where Rowdy's papers were. As Kevin had said, Ron had more or less known about the will.

"You know, he told me, Holly," he said. "But, you know, things change. He could've altered the will anytime. And I never saw the thing. I just heard plans. And I didn't want to see anybody let down."

"Roger must be more than a little let down," I said. "Or did he know?"

"He must've. Frank wasn't the kind of guy who'd lead him on like that."

Ron's line was that we'd all misjudged Roger. We all knew that since Dr. Stanton's sight had started to go, Roger had been doing most of his driving for him. We also knew that Roger had been doing a lot of other things for his uncle, keeping him company, sitting through long Sunday dinners. Is there a nice way to say this? We questioned Roger's apparent altruism. We felt that his motives might not be entirely disinterested. In particular, we doubted the sincerity of his interest in obedience training, mainly because we could all see that the only time he trained Lion was in class on Thursday nights. In short, we assumed he was sucking up to his rich uncle.

Ron didn't have Rowdy's papers and suggested I do what I would have done next anyway, namely, look in Dr. Stanton's library. Dr. Stanton's house is only a few blocks from mine, and for the posh end of Appleton Street, it's a small house. It's very Cambridge, what the Harvard types call Cantabrigian, a little English cottage. Rowdy needed to go out anyway, and I thought Millie might like to see him, so I leashed him and walked up the street. Millie had been with Dr. Stanton for a long time, and in the last year, he'd alternated between complaining about her and worrying about her. The complaint was that she fussed over him too much, and he claimed to be worried about her health, although it's my impression that tiny women like Millie live to a hundred. I'd sometimes wondered whether she didn't resent the extra work of having people come to use the library, but I asked Dr. Stanton about it once, and he said that it was part of her job and that someone else did all of the housework for her anyway.

When I rang the bell, I wondered what would happen to her now, how small the legacy was, whether she had somewhere to go. I assumed, however, that she would still be in the house, and I was right. She answered the door and, as usual, shuffled rapidly in reverse to let me in. Her back was even more bent than usual, from osteoporosis, I suppose, and she barely needed to lean over to give Rowdy the kiss that was apparently their routine greeting. He must have nearly outweighed her, and watching the two of them, I was reminded of those corny posters of a St. Bernard or a Great Dane with a fluffy, beribboned white kitten. After he lapped her face, she extended a hand to him, waved it up and down, and solemnly shook the paw he dutifully raised. I hadn't known he knew the trick.

"He's a good boy," she said to me. "He's very gentle."

"He *is* a good boy," I said. "I'll take good care of him."

She started to cry, and we spent a long time talking about Dr. Stanton. We had tea and graham crackers in the kitchen—lime green, redone in the fifties—and she told me all about how worried she'd been about Dr. Stanton, how worried he'd been, how he'd been so much better in the last week.

"And me thinking his ship must have come in," she said.

"He couldn't have been worried about money," I said.

Evidently, he had been, or that was Millie's story.

"Everything's so dear these days," she said, and I could imagine what had happened. One of them must have gone down the street to Formaggio, bought a round loaf of sourdough, and been charged two twenty-five. When whichever one it was came back, the two of them had had a long chat about how bread used to cost five cents a loaf, and Millie had taken the episode seriously. I wondered how much Dr. Stanton had paid her.

After I'd sat with her for a while, I asked to use the library, and she let me in. The first time I ever saw it, I thought that it must have been the reason Dr. Stanton bought the house, but when I learned that he'd had the library wing built, I could see that it was an addition to the cottage. What I liked best, besides the books, was the wood—wood bookshelves on all four walls, a warm wood ceiling, the oak floor, the maple desk. And, of course, the books and films and videotapes were a scholar's paradise: obedience books by Pearsall and

Leedham, Strickland, Koehler, everyone; Peary's journals of sled dog expeditions; *This Is the . . . , Meet the . . . ,* and *The Complete . . .* everything from affenpinscher to Yorkshire terrier; plus stud books, back issues of the breed quarterlies, veterinary journals, *Dog's Life, The American Kennel Gazette.* Furthermore, in a city that probably has more libraries per capita than any other place in the world, this was the one library in Cambridge where you could take your dog. Rowdy was, of course, perfectly at home. He denned up behind a big leather chair and fell asleep.

I often went to Dr. Stanton's to poke around and find a few books to borrow, but that day, I checked the walls. If Rowdy's pedigree were hanging up, I thought, I would have noticed it before, but I checked anyway. As I'd remembered, though, there were only a couple of prints of hunting dogs, so I went to the desk, which was where Millie thought Rowdy's papers would be. There, near the phone, the appointment book, and a pen set, was a photo of Rowdy on a snowy lawn, but that was it. Although Millie had given me the key to the file drawer on the lower right of the desk, the drawer wasn't locked, and the manila folder marked with Rowdy's name contained a complete record in Dr. Stanton's handwriting of Rowdy's checkups and immunizations, plus some more photos, a certificate of rabies vaccination dated about a year ago, a Cambridge dog license certificate, and a policy issued by the Animal Health Insurance Agency.

"You're up to date on your shots, big boy, and you don't have heartworm," I said. "But your papers aren't here."

Before we left, I signed out Riddle and Seeley's *The Complete Alaskan Malamute* and the malamute stud book, which lists more than you ever wanted to know about every Alaskan malamute ever registered with the American Kennel Club: sex, date of birth, registration number, color, sire, dam, breeder, owner, and more.

Roger Singer, I knew, would probably know where the papers were. Roger, however, was not someone I was eager to call, partly because I still had some lurking idea that he might try to take Rowdy, but mostly because he'd asked me out three or four times, and I'd always said no. Forgive a coarse analogy: an all too common behavior problem in male dogs is the habit of directing obvious sexual attention to pieces of furniture, people's legs, and such. Need I say more? Roger had always reminded me of those dogs, and I'm not sure why because, if anything, he probably struck most people as rather asexual. All I can say is that even though he knew about Steve, I didn't want to do anything that might sound like an invitation.

I called him anyway, offered my condolences, and asked about the papers. He was perfectly wholesome and unhelpful.

"Didn't you know? Rowdy doesn't have papers. He's a rescue dog."

I didn't believe it. A rescue dog? Maybe. But no papers? I knew, of course, that Rowdy was no puppy when Dr. Stanton got him. That was a little more than a year ago, and Rowdy had looked about ten months old. I'd also heard Dr. Stanton say that Rowdy was adopted, and I'd always assumed that he'd been returned to a breeder. Unlike a pet shop, a responsible breeder will take back a dog that has a problem—health, temperament, anything. Breeders also find themselves taking back full-grown dogs. A couple buys a dog. They split up, fight over the dog, and decide to put it to sleep unless the breeder takes it back. These things really happen. Rowdy obviously hadn't been returned for any health problem, so my guess was that he'd been too rambunctious for his first owner or that he'd been a casualty of a failing relationship. It never occurred to me that he'd been rescued. For one thing, a lot of rescued dogs have been abused, and he just didn't act like a dog with a history of abuse. For another thing, the dogs that end up with rescue societies tend to be pet shop dogs, and he looked to me, and to Buck, of course, like somebody's prize show dog—in fact, like a dog from the kind of kennel where you'd expect Dr. Stanton to buy a dog. Finally, although I knew Dr. Stanton had stopped showing, it hadn't crossed my mind that he'd have taken a dog without papers, a dog he'd never have the option of showing in breed or using as a stud.

One thing Roger did tell me was the name of Dr. Stanton's lawyer, and on Sunday, I managed to reach the guy, who was probably less than pleased to be called at home.

"I'm looking for his dog's papers," I said.

"Just use anything," he said. "They don't care. Or better yet, take him right outside. Keep taking him to the same spot. He'll get the idea."

"No, no. His AKC registration papers. A form from the AKC. And a pedigree, too, probably."

"Are they valuable?"

"Not exactly. But to Dr. Stanton, I'm sure they were. I thought he might've left them with you. Or in a safe-deposit box?"

"Sorry. If he had, I'd know."

I made some coffee and got out the stud book and the paper onto which I'd copied the tattoo, WF818769. The coffee was to keep me awake—unless you're deep into pedigrees, a stud book's plot is hard to follow—but I saw right away that I wouldn't need it. The last listing went from Adaka's Frosty Night to Ziljo's Antar-Tica, December of 1986, just about when Rowdy must have been born, much too early for his registration to appear.

For someone who raises wolf dogs, my father is a reactionary when it comes to the American Kennel Club. He wants wolf dogs recognized as a breed. (Actually, the AKC now recognizes them for what they are: interesting wild animals.) Buck knows that they won't be admitted soon, but he says that he's planning for the future. The planning seems to consist of ingratiating himself with the powers that be in the American Kennel Club. Or maybe, like a wolf, he's a creature of the pack, and the AKC has been his pack for so long now that he can't change his allegiance. For whatever reasons, he still knows a lot of people at the AKC, and if he wants something expedited there, he knows people who will help. A lot of those people, I suspect, remember Marissa. I called Buck with the registration number, and since the AKC wouldn't be open until the next day, he promised to call them and get back to me.

In the afternoon, I walked Rowdy back up Appleton Street to get Brearley's *This Is the Alaskan Malamute* from Dr. Stanton's library. Since I was there anyway, I fished around in the desk. The library was always open to everyone, so I didn't feel sneaky. Dr. Stanton wouldn't have kept anything personal in the desk, and I was still convinced that the papers were there somewhere. I found something, but not the papers. Maybe I shouldn't have read the appointment book, but I did. He had quite a few things listed for the week he died and the week after. On Friday, the day after he died, there were three appointments.

"Nine A.M. Sorenson, cleaning," I read aloud to Rowdy. The dentist? The guy who did the housework? "Noon. M.R. And four, our paper-training lawyer."

Kevin or the state police had probably checked up on everything. Millie had told me the police had spent hours here. I signed out the malamute book and a couple of recent issues of the *Malamute Quarterly,* called good-bye to Millie, and let myself out.

Buck didn't phone until late the next afternoon.

"Rowdy," said Buck, "is Snowcloud Kotzebue Thunderking."

When people hear names like that, they sometimes say things like, "Oh, so his real name is Snowcloud." Not so. If a puppy eventually becomes an international champion, the breeder wants the kennel name to share the glory. If Rowdy hadn't been Snowcloud Kotzebue Thunderking, he'd still have been Snowcloud something, or something of Snowcloud. If my parents had had high expectations for me, I'd be Winterland's Holly.

"And?" I said.

"And the breeder is Janet Switzer."

He paused. I knew something funny was going on.

"And," he continued, "the registered owner is one Margaret L. Robichaud."

"Jesus," I said. "Did you tell anyone at the AKC why you wanted that number looked up?"

He hadn't. He also pointed out that everyone knows what he breeds now. Anyone would assume that he was checking out a dog he wanted to use to produce hybrids, or checking out the bloodlines of a wolf dog. Besides, when Buck calls the AKC, people don't ask why he's calling.

Margaret's dead malamute licked my hand and woo-wooed at me to get off the phone.

Chapter 8

FOR the next two days I kept the information about Rowdy's registration to myself. I wrote an article about a man in Sudbury who uses Irish setters as sled dogs, got my hair cut, took Rowdy running, worked on his heeling, and thought about Margaret L. Robichaud.

I remembered all the squawking Margaret had done about the puppy. His name was King. Originality wasn't one of her strengths. According to Margaret, he was house-trained at ten weeks. Then she cured him of chewing. We heard about every obedience milestone from his heeling to his perfect recall. Meanwhile, of course, we saw nothing. There had even been jokes about Margaret's imaginary dog until she brought in photos. All I could remember about them was that one showed Margaret holding what was undoubtedly a malamute puppy. I looked at Rowdy, asleep on his side, legs stretched out, and I tried to match his face with the half-remembered blurry snapshot image I'd seen long ago. The pup, like Rowdy, had an open face—no dark markings on his muzzle or around his eyes—or so I thought. Otherwise? Otherwise, I didn't know. I also tried to fit Rowdy, Margaret, and Dr. Stanton into a single picture, even a blurry one, but someone always got left out or cut off. Had someone wanted Dr. Stanton cut out of the real picture?

I rechecked the registration number on Rowdy's tattoo, not hard to find now that I knew where to spread the fur. The numbers hadn't rearranged themselves. What had Stanton been doing with Margaret's dog? Had he even known that the dog was hers? After all, my eyesight was far superior to his, and I hadn't seen the tattoo until I gave Rowdy a bath.

On Wednesday I called Millie.

"This is Holly Winter. I've got a stupid question."

"Ask it," she said. She sounded lonely, glad to be asked anything.

"Did Dr. Stanton ever give Rowdy a bath?"

She laughed. "He tried once, when Rowdy first got here. I had such a time cleaning up that bathroom, and Rowdy never even got in the water."

"So what did Dr. Stanton end up doing? Did he have him groomed somewhere?"

"Oh, no," Millie said. "He always used a powder. Outdoors. A dry bath, he called it. But he didn't do it very often. Rowdy's a nice clean dog."

I hadn't thought of that. Malamutes are clean. They have less doggy odor than practically any other breed.

I had another question. "Could you tell me something? Where did he get Rowdy?"

"A lady brought him here," she said brightly. "The one with the corgis."

No one who'd worked for Dr. Stanton as long as Millie had could confuse corgis with Margaret's golden retrievers. Corgis stand about a foot high. They're sturdy, tough, bright little workers, and for a handler who likes spirit, they're great for obedience. I must have known forty women who could have been Millie's lady with the corgis.

"Do you remember her name?" I asked.

"I have no idea. She's a nice little thing."

No one, even Millie, would have called Margaret Robichaud a nice little thing. A mean big thing, yes, but Millie wouldn't have said it. Even before I talked to Millie, I'd known that Margaret hadn't given or sold Rowdy—King?—to Dr. Stanton. Harvard types like to talk about something called prosocial behavior. It's one of the things *Sesame Street* is supposed to teach. Maybe Big Bird would give or sell a dog to his archenemy, if he had one, but not Margaret L.

Robichaud. Admitting defeat is probably prosocial behavior. Strangling probably isn't. I pictured Margaret and Dr. Stanton on the lawn outside the armory. She loomed over him with the leash wrapped around her bony hands. Her elbows stuck out like the wings of an obese plucked goose. She was saying what she always said to us: "And if that doesn't work, jerk harder!"

But if Rowdy really was her dog, and if she wanted him back, why strangle Dr. Stanton? Why not just take Rowdy? And if she wanted Rowdy, why try to kill him, and me, too? Why let me keep him? Why let Dr. Stanton? If Margaret had gone to Stanton, shown him Rowdy's papers, pointed out the tattoo, and demanded him back, Dr. Stanton would have had a motive to kill *her,* of course, but he was dead and she was alive. Could there have been a struggle outside the armory? Steve had thought not, but Kevin might know something he was keeping to himself.

It's generally a good rule to avoid feeding two alpha males together. Circumstances sometimes demand exceptions to the rule. After a trip to the Fresh Pond Market that yielded three fat steaks, a bottle of Johnnie Walker Black, and four six-packs of Bud, I invited Kevin and Steve to dinner. Steve's mother and sister were in town, and they were all having dinner with old Dr. Draper, whose practice Steve had taken over, but Steve promised to stop by at ten or so when he was free. Once Kevin knew Steve wouldn't be there, he accepted.

Kevin seldom drinks hard liquor. I primed him with Johnnie Walker, then I pumped him. Except for his relationship with his mother, he's an attractive man—I like reddish hair and brawn—but I wasn't leading him on. He knew I was expecting Steve.

"Margaret Robichaud," I said over the steak. "I want to know where she was the night Dr. Stanton died."

"Mrs. Robichaud," Kevin said a little thickly, "was walking dogs."

"She only has one."

"She has four. Four dogs." He sounded put out. "Oh, excuse me. Four goldens. Margaret L. Robichaud was otherwise occupied in the daytime, and the four goldens required their walkies. Have I got that right?"

"Yes," I said. "I can see that you found her charming."

"I found her a pain in the butt," he said. "Pardon my French."

"And last Thursday?"

"Walkies. And did Mrs. Robichaud meet anyone while the doggies had their walkies?" Kevin's imitation of Margaret's anglicized Brattle Street drawl was not bad. "No, she didn't meet anyone. Has she ever taken Valium? She believes in saying no to drugs."

"Has she ever given it to the dogs? Did you ask her?"

He looked as if I'd asked him whether the goldens ever snorted coke.

"I'm not joking," I said. "Vets use it. Suppose you've got a male and you've also got a bitch that comes in season."

Kevin blushed.

"You put them in separate crates," I went on.

"Crates."

"Portable pens. Boxes. The things you see at the airport. Or in the back of a car."

"Cages," he said. He'd finished the steak, plus a baked potato and green beans. He was now on Budweiser, the great American truth serum.

"Crates. You put both of the dogs in crates, or you put them out in separate kennels, but what do you do about the noise? The male is going to be beating the sides of the crate or howling so all the neighbors complain. Solution? Doggy Valium."

Kevin gave his beer a suspicious look. He studied the can. Maybe he was wondering whether Budweiser sold a medicated variety to young women with overardent suitors.

"Or," I continued, "she might have used it if she shipped them by plane. Sometimes people sedate their dogs for plane travel so they don't get nervous."

"What's the story on that? Costs a bundle?"

"Showing dogs? Shipping them to shows? Costs a bundle." I nodded. "You pay plane fare for yourself and the dogs. Plus your hotel. Meals. That's why most people have RVs. Then there are entry fees, though they aren't much compared to the rest. You want some cake? Chocolate."

He did. Kevin believes in carbohydrate loading. He runs at Fresh Pond. The skinny Harvard types in their New Balance track suits take one look at him, sneer their genteel sneers, and streak ahead of him for the first half mile. He passes them, and he keeps passing them. Mrs. Dennehy attributes his success to a vegetarian diet.

"Of course," I said, "Margaret handles the dogs herself. She doesn't have any handler's fee."

A handler's fee is not small. And not only do you pay whatever the handler charges for showing the dog, you also pay travel and hotel expenses.

"But," I added, "keeping four dogs isn't particularly cheap, and she must have paid something for the new ones."

I was sure she'd bought them. I'd never known her to breed her own dogs. She'd always been the kind of person who arranges to have the pick of the litter, for which you pay a premium.

The Johnnie Walker was wearing off, or maybe it had been absorbed by the cake. Kevin's eyes looked a little sharper than they had before. I handed him another can of Bud.

"So she's loaded," he said, opening the can.

"No, not loaded. Not broke. Comfortable. Her family had a lot of money, but they weren't too pleased when she dropped out of college to get married. Or that's what I heard. I don't know whether they left her anything besides the house. The husband didn't have much, but maybe he had life insurance or something. She works. She does something at HCHP."

Harvard Community Health Plan is the biggest health maintenance organization in Boston. I'd never understood exactly what Margaret did there.

"Maybe she had access to pills there." He pointed to the steak bone left on his plate, then cocked his thumb in Rowdy's direction. "Mind if I give it to him?"

"Go ahead."

Rowdy, who'd been wandering around looking hopeful, snatched the bone from Kevin's hand and slunk off to a corner of the kitchen. Denned up there, grasping the bone between his front paws, gnawing on it, and raising his eyes to make sure we weren't going to try to take it back, he looked even more wolflike than usual. I wouldn't have wanted to try to take the bone away.

"HCHP doesn't leave Valium lying around," I said. "And she's not a doctor. She doesn't do anything really medical. She does, I don't know, patient education. Community relations. Something like that."

"And, in your opinion, what would a new dog have set her back?"

"I don't know," I said truthfully. "I don't know where she got them. I haven't seen them. I didn't even know she had them."

"Just say for a good one. Give me a ballpark number."

"For a likely show prospect? That's what she'd want. A thousand? More? For a real prize, a lot more. It all depends."

"Three, four thousand. Minimum."

"Probably more," I said. "Plus shots. Food. Where does she keep them?"

"Place is a little zoo," he said.

"Okay," I said. "Plus the cost of building runs. They're not that cheap."

"This is just for your ears," Kevin said. "Seven, eight months ago, Stanton started to spend big."

"Well, I can promise you he didn't spend anything on Margaret," I said. "He loathed her. Did you think he'd become her patron?" Her sugar daddy? The idea was grotesque. "What did he buy?"

"He withdrew cash," Kevin said. "Regular, large sums."

"And he worried about the price of bread," I said, but then

I remembered that I'd only imagined that. "Not necessarily bread, but Millie was saying he'd been, oh, under stress. She thinks he was worried about money, but, you know, I can't believe it."

"Believe it."

"He had an appointment with her," I said. "Margaret. But he died first."

"She had a letter from him. Showed it to me. I've got it. Said he'd be at her house. To have a talk. That's all. A couple of lines. According to her, she thought he wanted to patch things up."

"I don't believe it," I said, thinking about the tattoo. Kevin is a law enforcement officer. In the eyes of the law, a dog belongs to its registered owner. In my eyes, Rowdy belonged to me. If the registered owner goes to jail, who owns the dog? I had no idea, but I wasn't about to take the chance of turning Rowdy over to anyone, never mind a murderer. I looked at him curled up in his corner. The bone was gone. He hadn't just gnawed on it. He'd ground the whole thing up with his molars and swallowed it. I smacked my lips at him.

"Whose good boy are you?" I said.

The question just slipped out. I always used to ask Vinnie whose good girl she was. He rose, wagged his tail, ran to me, and offered me his big head to pat, ears flattened. I scratched the fur between his ears and thumped his back. He knew whose good dog he was.

It wasn't until about quarter of ten, when Kevin got up to leave, that I realized he must have been watching the clock. Rowdy stood up, shook himself, padded over to Kevin, and flopped on the floor, tummy up, legs in the air, and eyes expectant.

"You don't have to go. Steve would be glad to see you," I said. "Besides, I want to hear about Hal."

Kevin knelt down, dug his fingers into Rowdy's neck, shook him gently, then rubbed his tummy.

"You ought to get another dog," I said.

"Naw. It was awful when I lost Trapper. I couldn't go through that again," Kevin said, shaking his head.

"And Hal?"

"I've got some news about that character."

"What?"

"It'll keep," he said.

Steve arrived a few minutes after ten.

"Johnnie Walker Black," he commented, glancing at the bottle.

"I don't fool around."

"I hope not."

He'd left India at home. According to the monks of New Skete, your dog should sleep in your bedroom. Sleeping in your room gives the dog a chance to spend long relaxed hours near you, breathing your scent. Those long relaxed hours make for good canine mental health. The monks' advice proves that they don't cheat on their vow of celibacy. Besides, they don't keep malamutes. About half an hour after Steve arrived, Rowdy stretched his neck toward the bedroom ceiling and sang a series of yowling howls. We put him in the kitchen and locked the bedroom door. There are limits.

In the morning, I told Steve about Rowdy's tattoo and about Margaret, and he pointed out something I'd realized even before I pumped Kevin. Everything would have made sense if Dr. Stanton had murdered Margaret. He adopts Rowdy. She recognizes Rowdy. She knows about the tattoo. She blackmails Stanton. He wants to keep Rowdy and stop paying blackmail, and he hates her anyway. He strangles her. But, according to Kevin, there had been no struggle.

"What makes you think she recognized him? Didn't he get Rowdy after she left?" Steve was eating scrambled eggs and English muffins. It's the only hot breakfast I know how to cook, and fortunately, it's also Steve's idea of a real meal. If we had more time together, his cholesterol count would be sky-high. Buck met Steve in early October, when Buck was in town to do something about wolves for the Museum of Science. "Steve's a regular guy," he said with approval. "I mean, he likes to fish and hunt." Besides fishing and hunting, regular guys eat eggs for breakfast.

"Margaret got fired in the early summer," I said. "Supposedly, King died in August, or maybe it was early September. Dr. Stanton got Rowdy around the beginning of October, I think, maybe a little before. A year ago. You know, it's possible she's never seen him, though she could have seen him around here. She lives on Avon Hill. But she wouldn't have seen him at a show. He didn't show Rowdy."

"And now we know why."

"Now we think we know why. No papers. Damn it! I mean, Stanton had quit going to shows anyway, but I'm thirty years old, and I'm not ready to retire. And look. When you show up in obedience with a malamute, everyone thinks, you know, that it's sort of a joke. I mean, everyone says, 'Hm, willful and stubborn.' But Rowdy is different."

"So just get an ILP number."

That stands for Indefinite Listing Privilege. An ILP number would have let me show Rowdy in obedience, but not in breed, and it definitely wouldn't have made him my dog.

"Because Margaret could have the ILP cancelled anytime she felt like it. Damn it, I want to keep him."

"Has it occurred to you that Margaret wasn't necessarily the only person who could have made that connection? Between Rowdy and her dog? For a start, you did. Did anyone else?"

"Who?"

"Anyone who saw the tattoo."

"It's practically invisible," I said. "Unless you know it's there."

"Who was Stanton's vet?"

"Dr. Draper. I know because there was a rabies certificate in the file, the one in the library."

"I'll check the chart. Maybe Draper saw something and made a note."

"He wouldn't have done anything about it?"

"Why? Stanton was just the kind of guy who has his dog tattooed. Responsible, knows about tattoos, loves the dog. You see a tattoo, you assume the owner knows it's there. Why say anything?"

"Okay, check the chart," I said. "But don't ask Dr. Draper. Don't say anything to anyone. I almost didn't tell you. And also, I keep thinking that maybe Stanton did have the papers. You know, the AKC isn't the fastest organization in the world. When you register a dog, it takes a month or so to get the papers. I've been thinking that the registration might have been transferred, but it isn't on their books yet."

"That's wishful thinking," Steve said. "I'll check his chart today. I've got to go. I'll call you."

I started a column about cures for digging. It was on my mind. Rowdy was starting to turn my yard into a scale model of Verdun. Steve called at noon.

"I've checked the chart," he said. "There's nothing about the tattoo, but there is something you ought to know about. According to this, he's overdue for everything except rabies."

"There must be some mistake." I'd seen Dr. Stanton's record.

"Maybe he switched vets. People do."

"You don't just change vets for no reason."

"Oh, is that right?" Steve's was the voice of experience.

"Stanton would have made some note in the file," I said. "There's something fishy here. When was he due?"

"Let's see, September. A year from when we first saw him. And, oh, you might want to think about kennel cough. He got his heartworm test a little early, March. That was negative. You've been giving him the pills?"

Millie had given them to me. They were the old-fashioned kind, the little pink ones that you give every day from April through November. They were protecting Rowdy from heartworm, but not from anything else. They hadn't protected either of us against an overdose of Valium. A dog who loves everyone and who'll eat anything is vulnerable, even a big dog who looks like a wolf. Steve could protect him from distemper and leptospirosis and parainfluenza, but it was up to me to defend him against human beings.

Chapter 9

STEVE found ten minutes for us early that afternoon. Most dogs especially hate the shot for kennel cough, which isn't a shot at all. It's a nasal spray. I held Rowdy tightly while Steve loaded a hypodermic and squirted the contents into Rowdy's nose. Rowdy didn't budge. He didn't whine. He didn't struggle. He just took it. The real shots didn't faze him, either. Malamutes are highly desirable as laboratory animals. They have a high tolerance for pain. If I ever murder anyone, it will be some piece of scum who takes advantage of that toughness, that dignity.

Back home, I called Roger at work—some computer software outfit—and told him I had a few questions about Rowdy. He said he'd be home at four and invited me to stop in. I accepted. I'd bring Rowdy along to avoid being alone with Roger. The only way to straighten out the mess of Rowdy's papers, the only way to guarantee that I could keep him, the only way to make sure that no one ever slipped him any more Valium was, I'd finally realized, to find out what the hell was going on, and Roger was the logical place to start. If anyone knew who the lady with the corgis was, it was Roger. Besides, although I had no intention of telling him about the tattoo, I wanted to know just how much he'd had to do with Rowdy, how much chance he'd ever had to find the tattoo the way I'd found it. And, of course, I wanted to know the same thing Kevin had wanted to know about Margaret, whether there was any sign of a recent upswing in his income.

Washington Street runs from near Central Square toward MIT and the river. Shall we say that it's not Brattle Street. It took me ten minutes to find a legal parking space. If you park in a tow zone in Cambridge, a truck from Pat's Towing hauls your car away, and you have to pay all of your old tickets before you're allowed to retrieve the car from Pat's. The paint was peeling from Roger's brown triple-decker. The urine smell in the hall hadn't been left by Lion. Canine females don't spray. Human males do. Rowdy liked Roger's hallway. Dogs place no value on hygiene. Or maybe they do—the worse, the better.

Lion was barking so loudly that I knew Roger's apartment had to be the first on the left. The door opened a crack, then Roger's and Lion's big black-haired heads jutted out. Lion pushed open the door, and the dogs sniffed and wagged tails at each other.

"Friends, Lion," Roger commanded her firmly, as if she were showing signs of imminent attack. "Friends. Easy. It's all right, girl."

She was barking out a welcome and drooling. If dog drool offends you, don't get a Newfoundland. With better manners than Roger, she ran into the apartment and wagged an invitation to follow. Rowdy accepted.

"Come on in, Holly," Roger finally said.

The place had a thick, musty smell, like an airtight clothes hamper full of damp towels and dirty socks. Rowdy wiggled all over, and he and Lion dashed through an open door into what I could see was the kitchen, which probably smelled even better than the living room. Yum.

Like about half the apartments in Cambridge, Roger's had white everything—walls, woodwork, curtains, rug, Haitian cotton couch, tub chairs from Crate and Barrel. But Roger's decor reflected the presence of a Newfie. Layers of black fluff coated everything. Lion had sculpted artful carvings into the baseboards and legs of the oak coffee table. It was a cozy little place.

Roger disappeared into the kitchen, where the dogs were

probably working on some new interior-decoration plan, and he reappeared with a bottle of Massachusetts wine and two glasses. Many people don't think of Massachusetts as a great wine-producing region, and they're right. He poured me a glass. I held it near my mouth. Maybe I'd been wrong about the smell in the hall.

"So you going to dog training tonight, Holly?"

"Of course," I said. "Do I ever miss?"

"You okay now?"

"Fine. Rowdy, too."

There was an awkward silence during which I decided that Roger actually looked more like a gorilla than a Newfoundland, the kind of gorilla that sits in its cage at the zoo and inspires kids to ask their parents embarrassing questions.

"Now that I've got Rowdy," I said, "I wondered if you could tell me a couple of things about him."

"Giving you a hard time, huh?"

From Roger's point of view, the purpose of my visit was obviously to ask his advice about dog training.

"I just wondered where he came from, and I thought you might know. Millie said something about a woman with corgis."

"Oh, her," Roger said. "Roberta Reed. Lives out in Pepperell, Dunstable, one of those places. Dog went on some rampage and ended up with her."

I knew Bobbi Reed.

"What was she doing with a malamute?"

"It was one of those rescue operations. She was an old friend of Uncle Frank's, and she talked him into it. Beautiful dog, too bad to see him put to sleep, the usual."

Dr. Stanton was not the kind of person who gets talked into things, but I didn't say so.

"What kind of shape was he in? When your uncle got him?"

"Uh, not bad. Thin."

"And his coat?"

"Not bad."

"I tried to give him a bath, but I didn't have much luck," I said. "I wondered if there was some knack to it. I thought maybe when Dr. Stanton first got him, you might've given him a hand." There. I'd asked for advice. Some men aren't happy unless you do.

"No," Roger said, and started to say more when a noise came from the kitchen, the sound of an object being dragged across the floor.

"They're up to something," I said.

Something was a forty-pound bag of Science Diet dog food, or, should I say, a bag that had once held forty pounds of Science Diet. I was a little surprised to see it. I'd figured Roger for the supermarket generic type. Roger had carried the color scheme from the living room over into the kitchen, but he'd worked even harder to personalize it there. His most effective decorator touch was a free-form smoke-gray abstract over the stove.

"Oh, damn. I'm so sorry," I said as I leashed Rowdy and hauled him away from the open bag. It took all the strength I had. Northern breeds are better adapted for hauling than for being hauled.

"Happens all the time," Roger said cheerfully, pushing Lion away from the bag and adding, probably for my benefit, "Lion, shame, bad girl."

As he put his hand on her collar, I noticed that it was her metal chain link training collar, the kind you never, ever leave on a dog. I also noticed that it was on the wrong way. If you put the collar on right, it tightens when you pull on the lead, and it releases the second you let go. If you put it on wrong, it tightens, but it doesn't release.

"You ought to take that collar off," I said. "She could get it caught on something and choke."

Roger said that he must have forgotten.

"Oh," I said as I headed toward the door, "I meant to ask you something else. Where did Rowdy get his shots this year?"

"Draper, I guess." His jowly face looked blank.

"Dr. Stanton didn't have some kind of argument with Dr. Draper? He wasn't unhappy about something?"

"No. Nothing."

"You didn't take Rowdy in for him?"

"Uncle always did that. Didn't like to recognize, uh, how he was failing."

"How did he get there? I mean, he didn't drive?"

I knew, of course, that Dr. Stanton hadn't driven for a couple of years. His sight was too bad.

"Took a cab, I guess."

With a ninety-pound dog?

It turned out that Bobbi Reed lived in Dunstable, which is right off Route 3, near the New Hampshire border. I called and told her that I wanted to do an article about corgis, and we set up a visit for the next day. Since it was Thursday, I went to dog training. The patrols were out, and we'd also hired a security guard. The prospect of Dr. Stanton's legacy was already helping.

On the way home, I was surprised to spot Hal on Concord Avenue, not far from the armory. After Kevin's cryptic remark, I'd assumed Hal was still locked up somewhere, but there he was, as usual, fishing around at the base of a tree, probably looking for cans and bottles. Rowdy was heading for the same tree, but I held him back, not that Hal was sober enough to have cared.

"Hi, Hal," I said. I spend my spare time dreaming up slick openers like that.

Hal mumbled something.

"What?"

He mumbled again. I thought I heard him say something about me. Something obscene. Maybe I was right. His articulation suddenly improved. "Don't say that!" he yelled. "You're not supposed to say that."

Dark as it was, I could see him look right through me before he meandered off toward the armory.

* * *

On Friday morning, I put Rowdy in the Bronco and took Route 2 to 128, then 3 North. Bobbi Reed and Ronni Cohen used to live in Cambridge. In those days, Bobbi was active in the club, but she quit when they moved. The drive from Dunstable to Cambridge is less than an hour, and Bobbi doesn't lack energy, so maybe the move was an excuse to find a trainer other than Margaret Robichaud. Since the move, I'd run into Bobbi at a couple of shows, and she'd told me that she was breeding corgis. She'd always had a couple of them. One of her specialties was brace work. A brace is a pair of dogs of the same breed. In obedience, they do all the usual exercises, but the two dogs work together with one handler. When they heel, they both walk on the handler's left side, and so on. When it's done well, it's a flashy performance.

Bobbi is about five feet tall. Even for dog training, she always wore lots of scarves, and she liked the jewelry you buy at the Peabody Museum Shop: Navajo necklaces, Peruvian beads. That ethnic look suits someone with her dark hair. She used to be a nun. That was before she met Ronni and developed ecumenical fervor, in more ways than one. Ronni's parents welcomed Bobbi the way the Church welcomed Ronni. Bobbi left the Church, and she and Ronni moved to Cambridge, where no one cared. Most of the dog people didn't notice. In Cambridge, most people are interested in whether you shave your legs as a political statement and what you think about Wittgenstein. Obedience people are interested in how careful you are on your turns. I wondered whether Dunstable cared. If it ever had, I would bet it didn't anymore, because Bobbi had probably found a way to build a new library without raising taxes while organizing the harvest festival in her spare time. She was the treasurer of the Cambridge Dog Training Club before Ron Coughlin, and she was also the planning genius of our big annual obedience trial.

Bobbi's directions took me to a back road. Dunstable doesn't have any major ones. The pines reminded me of Owls

Head. When Bobbi said she was breeding corgis, I should have realized that she didn't mean raising a litter or two. When I pulled into the drive, I saw six or eight long runs and a large pen on the left, with one or two dogs in each. On the right, in a rustic log corral, a Morgan horse stared at me and swished his tail. Ahead was a split-level probably built in the fifties, now cedar-shingled and trying to earn the name ranch.

Ten or twelve dogs constitute an automatic doorbell. Bobbi and two corgis appeared at the side of the house. All of hers were Pembrokes. The easiest way to tell Pembroke and Cardigan Welsh corgis apart is that Pembrokes have their tails docked as short as possible. Cardigans have tails. Pembrokes are also shorter and have pointed ears, and there are a few other differences, too, but they're indiscernible unless you're used to corgis. One of the ones with Bobbi was called Brandy, I remembered, short for some unpronounceable Welsh name that was all *w*'s. Brandy's buddy looked like him, reddish with white feet, almost certainly a son.

"This place is fantastic! I had no idea," I said.

"We're getting there," she said. "It's been a lot of work. When we bought it, the house had turquoise siding, and there were actually pink flamingos on the lawn. Can you believe it? The mal looks great. You keeping him? He's a real sweetheart."

He and Brandy and the other loose corgi were chasing one another around the house, veering and pouncing. The house and kennels were enough to make me think about leaving Cambridge. My second-floor tenant, Rita, says that the inability to leave Cambridge reflects endlessly protracted adolescence. It actually reflects the unwillingness to quit wearing jeans. Maybe Rita's right. Therapists sometimes are, I guess.

The kitchen had a restaurant-style range, a picture window with bird feeders hanging outside, and blue-and-white-patterned wallpaper. Wallpaper. If Harvard had its way, the Cambridge zoning regulations would prohibit wallpaper inside city limits. Maybe they already do. Bobbi had outgrown

Cambridge. After I asked her a lot of questions about corgis and half filled a steno pad with her answers, I got to the point of the visit, Rowdy.

"Well, he was such a love," she said. "And there was Frank, getting old, eyes going, and I talked to him about a puppy. He was here for a meeting, a big deal, planning the Northern Mass. show. Bronwyn had a litter then, and he liked corgis, but housebreaking was an issue. If it had been some other malamute, I would have thought twice about it. A malamute is really a young person's dog, I always think. So the long and the short of it is that after the meeting, I brought the mal in, and, of course, Rowdy sold himself."

Rise up a little on your hind legs. Cross your front paws and place them in the victim's hands. Fold your ears against your head. Gaze imploringly. Smile.

"The big-brown-eyes routine," I said.

"You got it. So Frank said he'd think it over. Naturally, he called me the next day, and I drove Rowdy in."

"Where'd the name come from?"

"Frank. That was his. We just called him King."

I nearly dropped the blue and white teacup.

"You know," Bobbi said, "Sergeant Preston. Don't you remember? On, King! On, you huskies!"

The real reason I should leave Cambridge is that I'm not too bright. I'd missed the connection. I knew, of course, that on the old TV show, King was a malamute. There was even a picture in one of the malamute books I'd just been reading, by Brearley. Margaret must have known, too. Bobbi and Ronni? What had they really known? Nothing? Calling a stray malamute King is like calling a stray collie Lassie. It doesn't have to mean anything.

"I remember," I said. "Yukon King, the Wonder Dog. How did you end up with him? Isn't he a little big for a corgi?"

"Jim Tuttle talked me into boarding him. From the Siberian Rescue League?" She meant Siberian huskies, of course, not Soviet defectors. "You know him?"

"Sure. He does the sled dog demonstrations."

"Right." She pushed her hair out of her face and smiled. "They got him from a guy in Pepperell, some guy who keeps chickens, believe it or not. An incredibly nice guy. Most people would've got a gun and that would've been it. He lost six chickens. Anyway, Rowdy lucked out. He must have been starving, poor baby."

The other chickens lucked out, too, I thought. Only six. A loose dog, especially a malamute, can kill hundreds in no time. (By the way, don't think that shipping your wild-acting dog to a farm is going to solve any problems. In the city, there aren't any deer, sheep, or cows to run down. There aren't any chickens, geese, or ducks to kill. There aren't any farmers with guns to protect their livestock. If your dog acts wild, don't deport him. Train him.)

"More tea?" Bobbi asked.

"Sure," I said. "So the guy thought he was a Siberian."

"Right. So the Siberian people took one look and saw what he was. You know there's finally a malamute protection league starting?"

"I heard about it."

"It's new. Anyway, Jim called me and asked if I could board a malamute for a while, and you know what I'm like." I did—softhearted. "And they advertised, but who knows? For one thing, he could've come from anywhere. A few hundred miles is nothing to a dog like that."

Who knew? I did, or I thought I did. I wasn't about to say so.

"Tell me something," I said. "Did you give him a bath?"

"Did you?" She laughed.

"Yes. I have the scars."

"Good for you. Ronni tried, and we ended up tying him up outdoors and turning the hose on him. Then we just let him loose in the big pen to dry off. I'd bathe and groom twenty corgis before I'd try that again. I knew some malamutes were like that, but I'd never seen it before."

"Speaking of malamutes," I said, trying to sound normal,

"whatever happened to the one Margaret Robichaud had? Do you know about that?"

"Do I ever know about that. Did I ever hear about that. Did she ever talk about that. We worked on something together just after it happened. She was really broken up, and when Margaret's broken up about something, she talks."

"So what was the story?"

"Well, she took him to Maine, and he bolted somehow, right at the end of her vacation. They always know. So she did everything, ads in the papers, called everyone, and finally she got hold of some shelter in Maine that had picked him up. He'd been hit by a car."

"A car?"

"I think so. Anyway, he was in bad shape, and he didn't make it. It must have been awful for her."

"Terrible," I said. I felt like a hypocrite. Maybe it *had* been terrible.

"I had nightmares after she told me about it," Bobbi said. "Brandy's body was stretched out on a slab in a sort of morgue with white tiles, and these ghoulish people were around, and they kept asking me, 'Is this your dog?' "

"Did Margaret actually see him?"

"I don't think so," Bobbi said. "I'm not sure. I think somebody gave her some gruesome description of his body. I think that's what gave me the dreams."

Before I left, I slipped in a question about whether Bobbi had ever seen Margaret's King. She said no, and I believed her.

Massachusetts does not look its best in November in the rain. Everything turns a dead, sodden brown-gray. All the way home I kept thinking about Margaret and feeling guilty. If she'd known that her dog was still alive, would she have talked to Bobbi like that? Wouldn't she have said nothing? I know what it's like to lose a dog. One of the ways people console themselves is to talk to anyone who'll listen. Kevin's dog died years ago, and he still does it. From Bobbi's account, Margaret had sounded like someone whose dog has died, or at least like someone who thinks that her dog has died.

It seemed to me that Bobbi hadn't seen that tattoo, and I didn't think that Ronni had, either. The name King bothered me, but it didn't bother me a lot, and they weren't the only people who could have made the connection between Rowdy and Margaret. Old Newfie Roger was still a possibility, for a start, and so was old Dr. Draper, whatever Steve might think. Much as I'd always liked Ron Coughlin, I wondered about the trip to the men's room, too, the way Kevin did. I also wondered about the tattoo, and I wondered whether it was the only way to connect Rowdy to Snowcloud Kotzebue Thunderking.

Chapter 10

I MISSED Marissa something fierce. I could imagine picking up the phone and telling her what any reasonable mother wants to hear: "Mom, he finished thc last leg. I've got a Utility malamute." It wasn't that Buck wouldn't care. He'd announce it to everyone. He'd glow. But he's not my mother.

But I was a long way from Utility—in fact, a C.D., a C.D.X., the three legs of a U.D., and one set of registration papers away—and I still had no idea of what was going on. I took a deep breath, pretended I was Rowdy having a hypodermic shoved up my nose, and called Margaret Robichaud.

"Something reminded me of you the other day," I said. "Actually, it was something on *Sesame Street.*"

"You must be joking."

"No. Really," I said.

After that, she was more polite, more gracious than I would have been under the circumstances. The reason was not good manners, of course, or a liking for me. I told her I wanted to interview her for *Dog's Life.* There's nothing I won't do for a dog. I hadn't yet dreamed up a topic for the interview. Anything would do. A winner's tips on handling. Grooming secrets. She wouldn't care. She didn't even ask. Since she had a show on Saturday, I had until late Sunday afternoon to concoct something.

Steve and I had a romantic weekend together. On Saturday, we went to a Celtics game. Dogs are not my only interest. One of Steve's patients, or, should I say, the owners of one of his patients, had been so grateful to Steve for making a house call—difficult labor, mother dachshund and pups now resting comfortably—that they gave him two tickets for the game. You practically can't buy Celtics tickets. To get them at all, you need season tickets, and season tickets are like the crown jewels. You inherit them or marry for them, but you don't just buy them.

"Did you know they had season tickets when you made that house call?" I asked him as we sat in the Garden waiting for the pregame.

"Of course not," he said.

Larry Bird was out for surgery to remove bone spurs from both heels. The Celtics lost, but after the game we went to the Union Oyster House and fed each other cherrystones, and Sunday morning was so rainy that the dogs didn't start scratching on my bedroom door until ten. The rain had stopped by the time we finished our eggs and coffee. We drove to the Middlesex Fells and ambled through the damp woods with the dogs.

Margaret had always made me nervous, so when Steve dropped me off at home, I put on a navy corduroy Laura Ashley jumper and lace blouse. I wore tights and blue flats. I knew that Margaret would make me feel like a little girl, so I dressed for the part.

Here and there in Cambridge are old houses that look as if they were once farms. Quite a few are on Avon Hill, just north of what used to be the Radcliffe dorms, now Harvard houses, only a ten-minute walk from where I live. In an ordinary city, Avon Hill would be an ordinary neighborhood. In Cambridge, it's almost Brattle Street. Margaret's was one of the farmhouses, soft yellow with a bay window and, on one side, a white porch. I knew she lived alone. Her husband had died years ago. I rang the bell and heard dogs, but when Margaret opened the door, two goldens were lying quietly on the floor, not jumping or barking. I hadn't seen either of them before. They were beauties, with lovely heads and pale, shiny coats.

"Holly," she said. "I heard you lost your little golden. Cancer?"

Vinnie stood twenty-two inches at the withers and weighed sixty-five pounds, which is an ideal size for a golden retriever bitch. There was nothing little about her.

"Yes," I said, and changed the subject. "These young ladies are new, aren't they?"

"Cara and Missy. Missy's thirteen months, and she's got two majors. Cara went Best of Opposite in Worcester yesterday, and does she know it."

Braggart.

"They look beautiful," I said truthfully.

Margaret did not and never had. She'd looked almost exactly the same for as long as I'd known her, tall and graceless with large bones and what dermatologists around here call Yankee skin, pale with scaly red patches of sun damage. She'd probably had her hair done recently. It was a slightly copper brown swirled into some kind of chignon and pinned down tightly. She was wearing the same kind of outfit she'd always worn, a cream blouse that tied at the neck and a green and blue tweed suit probably intended to bring out the strange blue-green of her cat eyes.

"You're looking well yourself," I added brightly.

She thanked me and offered tea or coffee, which I refused. Steve had made me promise. We didn't sit in her living room but in a small study with a golden yellow carpet on which no fur showed, long matching curtains, bookcases filled with dog books and trophies, a handsome oak rolltop desk, two easy chairs elaborately upholstered in leaf-patterned chintz, and, on the off-white walls, displays of ribbons and framed photos taken at shows. The room was attractive but not opulent, and its only new contents were some of the ribbons, trophies, and photos. Margaret had released the dogs and permitted them to follow us, but as soon we entered the room, she downed them again.

I'd decided to avoid the topic of obedience in the interview, but I hadn't picked a substitute. I wasn't worried. I knew something would come up. The trophies and ribbons were from everywhere, so I asked about tips for traveling. How do you transport your dogs to shows? What problems do you encounter? Margaret was so used to being interviewed that I didn't have to do much except listen to her and scribble in a steno pad. I asked about motion sickness and medication. She said she'd never had any trouble and didn't believe in doping dogs. She talked about crates and airlines and motels. She knew her subject well. It seemed to me that in the past year, she'd hit every major show in the country and some in Canada. Unlike most show people, she hated RVs. For distant shows, she flew and then rented a station wagon. She interviewed herself, and I was a little chagrined to realize that her monologue would write up well.

After forty-five minutes, I asked about her other dogs, and she led me through an unrefurbished kitchen to the backyard. Although I'd heard her called horsy, she walked like a camel. The yard and kennels were superb. If I ever took up blackmail or extortion, I'd spend my gains duplicating that setup, except that I wouldn't have room. Margaret turned on floodlights that illuminated a yard about ten times the size of mine. On the left, against the wooden fence—the whole yard was enclosed—was a new building the size of a garage, with four concrete runs. On the lawn sat regulation-size jumps and hurdles, not just a high jump and the four hurdles for the broad jump, but also a barrier jump, a long jump, and a window jump. Margaret strode over to the little building and led me in. I'd always thought that Marissa's bathing and grooming area in the barn in Owls Head was ideal, but that was before I saw this one. The whole room was tiled in blue and white, but there was an area carpeted with matting that obviously gave her a place to train the dogs in bad weather. A heater and an air conditioner had been built into the wall. Everything was new. Kevin must not have seen this. The sunken tub was something you'd expect to find at the LaCoste Spa. If Margaret had tried to sell me a membership, I would have joined. This place gave the word *doghouse* a new meaning.

In two of the four pens along one wall were Margaret's two other goldens: Libby, the one I remembered, and a new one, a male, both barking and jumping in excitement.

"This is spectacular," I told her. I'd never before felt such simple covetousness. "It's fantastic."

What it wasn't was dog heaven. Rowdy would have been disappointed when he tried to dig through the concrete, and he would have found the total absence of odor a bore. It was, in fact, a doghouse for people, not dogs. I was jealous anyway.

Back in the study, she finally asked whether I had a new dog.

"I've got a malamute," I said.

"Oh, my dear," she gushed. "Let me give you some advice. You take that training collar, and you slip it high up on his neck. You don't have a bitch, do you?"

I said I didn't.

"You slip that collar high on his neck, and when he forges, you correct him for all you're worth. Goldens don't need it, but it's the only way, believe me." Dispensing advice, she sounded even more than usual like a malevolent Julia Child. I expected her to wish me *bon appétit* as if I intended to fork into malamute stew, but she actually wished me good luck with him and added, "You remember my mal, don't you? He was a lovely boy."

"I saw pictures," I said. "I was really sorry to hear."

"I was heartbroken," she said as she sat forward in the upholstered chair and pointed at me. "Devastated. All that work. I didn't have the heart to go through it again."

She reminded me of Kevin except that he was mourning his dog and she was mourning her own work.

To my surprise, she heaved herself even further forward and confided, "You know, I've started to think that it might have been a judgment on me for that silly controversy with

Frank. I feel terrible about him. Did you know he was coming to apologize?"

"I didn't know," I said. "I'm glad to hear it."

"He wrote to me," she said forcefully, as if I'd contradicted her. "Just before it happened. This is becoming a terribly violent society, isn't it?"

Who could disagree? If the purpose of my visit had been different from what it was, I might have pointed out that violence wasn't totally baffling when you considered that her dogs lived in most people's idea of a palace. I'm glad I didn't say it, especially because my dogs have always eaten better than most children do.

Without waiting for me to agree or disagree, she went on. "I knew Frank from girlhood. You didn't know that, did you? I had a brother, Bill. They were classmates." The unspoken phrase was *at Harvard.* "They served together."

At first I thought she meant that they'd been waiters, but I caught my mistake. "In World War II?"

"And the end of the war, and just after. The Navy," she said. Her face usually registered nothing besides arrogance, but the look of sadness softened her eyes. "Your mother knew Frank, didn't she?"

"Yes." Marissa knew everyone. Margaret said that Marissa was a better handler than Buck would ever be, and she asked about him.

"He's fine," I said. "I just saw him. He's still in Owls Head. You go to Maine, too, don't you? Deer Isle?"

I didn't slip the question in smoothly, but I slipped it in. Margaret didn't seem to notice. Some people never wonder why you're asking about them. They assume you're as interested as they are. Deer Isle was only a hunch.

"Blue Hill. We've always gone there."

Deer Isle. Blue Hill. Sailing. Tennis. Episcopalians. And, I admit, golden retrievers. I knew enough to realize that "we" wasn't, for once, the goldens, but three or four generations of her family. We talked about Maine. She reminded me to slip that training collar high on my dog's neck.

* * *

When I walked into my kitchen and turned on the overhead light, I saw that Rowdy had had fun in my absence. He'd managed to open a cabinet door that I must have left ajar, and he'd torn up and eaten what he found: boxes of cereal, crackers, and raisins. The worst mess was from a box of chocolate cake mix. Chocolate is bad for dogs. He and I discussed his behavior. I said that this was not my idea of Companion Dog behavior. I shook the packages in his face. I hoped that Rita was home in her apartment on the second floor. She thinks that it's good for people to express their feelings. Rowdy put his tail down and lowered his head. He never stopped watching me, and I think he listened. I was glad Margaret Robichaud wasn't there. I was glad Marissa wasn't there. The only thing worse than having your dog do something outrageous is having someone else find out about it.

When I'd vacuumed and was letting the floor dry, I sat on a stool and called Buck to ask about animal shelters and rescue places near Blue Hill. He gave me a few names. I also asked him to tell me again about malamutes and the U.S. Navy.

Chapter 11

ANYONE who loves dogs must wonder what the world looks like from the dog's point of view. When we wonder how the dog sees the world, we're already wrong because the dog doesn't so much see the world as sniff it and hear it. If dogs wonder about our world, they probably ask how it stinks and sounds to us, but our own first question isn't completely misguided. Dogs and people do see the world differently. For one thing, dogs are lower down than we are, so their perspective is lower than ours. For another, their visual world is mainly black and white and gray with some red. Black, white, and gray like sled dogs on an ice floe, red like that bomb exploding.

Buck hadn't, for once, known more than the books had already told me. In 1935, the American Kennel Club recognized the Alaskan malamute. The foundation stock consisted of the original Kotzebue dogs, and when there were enough of them, the AKC closed the stud book, which means that from then on, all registered malamutes were supposed to be descendants of the original ones. Without World War II and the Antarctic expeditions, the stud book would have stayed closed. In fact, having shown their capacity to do more than their fair share for Admiral Byrd, malamutes were summoned to do more than their fair share in World War II as well. Man's gratitude to dogs is such that it was fairly routine to thank the sled dogs at the end of an expedition by blowing them up or by leaving them behind to starve to death. Shortly after World War II, the commander of a U.S. Navy vessel in the Antarctic thanked a great many malamutes the speedy way. In 1947, there were only about thirty surviving registered Alaskan malamutes. Did the AKC train and dispatch commando teams to deliver appropriate thanks on behalf of the dogs? No. It reopened the stud book.

Did anyone avenge any of those dogs? Had someone waited forty years? Dr. Stanton? Where had he been in the years just after World War II? Obviously, he hadn't been massacring dogs, but had he known something? Recognized someone? Had someone wanted to silence him? Who else was old enough to have been in the Navy at that time? Ray Metcalf was old enough. Gerry Pitts probably was, too. Wouldn't the armory be managed by an old army man? Or could his military obsession with neatness—no dogs on the lawn—be a vestige of time in the Navy? Who had, in fact, been in the Navy? For one, Margaret's brother.

It hadn't occurred to me to ask Buck about him when we talked on the phone, but since my plans for the early part of the week included a visit to Owls Head, I didn't call back. This idea about the Navy seemed so improbable that I decided to pursue those plans, which called for finding out whether or not Margaret really believed that King had died. On Monday morning, I got out the list of animal shelters in Maine that Buck had dictated to me, and I called to schedule a series of visits. My pretext was, again, an article for *Dog's Life.* Pretext? I'd already started to draft something about corgis, and Margaret had done everything except put her tips for travel in writing.

By Monday afternoon, Rowdy and I were working our way up the Maine coast. We arrived in Owls Head at nine-thirty that night. Buck was in Vermont to barnstorm for wolves, so we didn't see him. No one was there except Regina Barnes, who must be at least eighty and is half mad. She used to confuse me with my mother even before Marissa died. She didn't like Marissa any more than she likes me. As the neighbors in Owls Head say, she has her cap set on Buck. He shouldn't take advantage of her hopes, but he does. He has a hard time finding people to wolf-sit. When I left in the morning, Regina was in the barn dispensing Science Diet. I called out to her, and I'm not sure who growled back.

At a shelter not far from Belfast, I nearly adopted a kitten that the guy swore was half Maine coon cat, but I didn't have a cat carrier with me, and the kitten's eyes were oozing some yellow glop. Everywhere I went, I had to turn down dogs. "There's an Irish setter back there," I'd hear, and in the cage would be a red dog with maybe one Irish setter grandparent. "Pointer" meant all spotted dogs except the really little ones. Those were fox terriers. Furry dogs with curly tails were huskies and half-huskies. I got offered one half-malamute. He was a big furry dog with a curly tail. A collie and shepherd mix meant a brown dog. I didn't mind. If a purebred name helped save one of them from those back-road death rows, who was I to get prissy about the AKC?

I heard a lot of sad stories. Animal rescue shouldn't have to mean gas chambers, but it usually does. If I ran the world, anyone who left a mixed breed bitch unspayed or a mixed breed dog unaltered would be taxed a few thousand dollars a year to help finance real shelters. So would anyone who let a purebred dog run free to help make more unwanted puppies.

By eight that night, when we checked in at the Ellsworth Holiday Inn, I was tired and depressed. Holiday Inns, by the way, are one of my own tips for travel with a dog. Some Holiday Inns don't let you keep a dog in your room, but lots of them do.

In the morning, we headed inland to Bangor and then back toward the coast. I'd managed to reach Buck in Vermont, and we'd arranged to have a short lunch at a diner on Route 1 near Union. He was walking Clyde when I pulled up. The dogs, of course, had to stay locked in the cars while we ate. Buck went to Europe once. All that he seems to have noticed is that in France, Italy, and Switzerland, dogs were welcome in restaurants. If hybridizing hadn't sidetracked him, he'd have organized a restaurant reform movement here.

Over fried clams and apple pie with cheddar cheese, we talked about Margaret. I was surprised. Buck doesn't usually use the words *prize bitch* metaphorically. I asked about her brother.

"Bill Lytton," he said, "had a pointer that was about the finest hunting dog you'd ever want to see. Field trial champion. Trained the dog himself. His sis was at every field trial, of course. You know, she antagonized a lot of people."

"Dear Margaret?"

"That snide attitude does not become you."

"Sorry."

"She wasn't so bad before Bill died. People got their backs up hearing her go on about him and Jack, that was all. That was the dog's name—Jack. It was only afterward, she developed this attitude. I heard somebody say about her the other day, her greatest dream is to die wrapped in her own arms."

Then he told me a lot more about the dog Jack and a few others. I tried to get him to say more about the brother, but either he'd never known much or he'd forgotten. He did, of course, know Frank Stanton, and he hadn't bothered to tell me before that Dr. Stanton had been in the Navy.

"Antarctica," he said when I raised my new hypothesis. "Just tell me. Why would the Navy send an eye doctor to Antarctica?"

"Snow blindness?" I answered, but I knew Buck was right. Medical specialization wasn't nearly so common in the 1940s as it is now, and even now, an ophthalmologist would be posted at a research center or a hospital, not shipped out on an icebreaker. Buck did give me one useful lead. He told me about a shelter that wasn't on my list, not a real shelter, just a place run by two brothers. It was nearby, on a dirt road between Union and Warren.

Union might sound familiar because of the fair. The Union Fair has horse pulling, tractor pulling, rides, beano, thick-sliced onion rings, and french fries served with vinegar. It hosts the Maine Blueberry Festival. The empty fairgrounds weren't very festive on that dark November afternoon. I took a right turn not far past them.

Without Buck's directions, I'd never have found the place, a collection of dog pens and rusted kitchen appliances and, behind a fence of burned-out trucks, shacks that in the thirties were overnight cabins. In these surroundings, the Bronco looked like a Rolls. I left Rowdy in it. This was no place for a classy dog.

My clothing budget is limited. A first-rate parka goes on my defense budget. I was wearing a new navy-blue Gore-Tex Maine warden's parka, $179.95 from L.L. Bean and worth it, especially in the gusts that slapped me as I made my way through the weeds from the Bronco to the closest shack. In front of the shack was an old Ford sedan, lime green when it left Detroit, now pitted and spotted brown like a child's stuffed dog about to lose its innards. Maine snow falls as white as snow anywhere else, maybe whiter, but it must corrode metal and flesh. The guy who answered my knock on the sagging door had taken a blizzard in the face.

"Hi," I said. "My name is Holly Winter. I'm Buck Winter's daughter. I'm looking for Roy or Bud."

Something told me that Roy and Bud didn't subscribe to *Dog's Life.* This scene looked more like Dog's Death.

"Roy Rogers," he said, holding out a hand that was overdue for a manicure. He was somewhere between thirty and eighty, and he wore some tan pieces of cloth that had once, I thought, been an army uniform. His brown-speckled face crinkled all over. His teeth matched his face. Poverty can rust your smile.

"I shook hands with Roy Rogers when I was seven years old," I said. That's true. I put a glove on that hand and refused to take it off for a week. "I didn't know I'd have a second chance."

I shook hands with this Roy Rogers, and he opened the door wide to let me in. An old wood stove was burning. It wasn't the kind you buy down the street from my house at Cambridge Alternative Power. Roy had no alternative.

There were two wooden chairs with peeling yellow paint. Everything else in the room was covered with cans of food, ragged blankets, old newspapers, iron frying pans, and bags and bags and bags of dog food. Roy sat on one of the chairs, and I got the place of honor, one end of a blanket-covered cot.

"So, the wolf man's daughter," he said.

I'd heard that about as many times as he'd been asked where Trigger was.

"That's right," I said. "He sent me here. Said that you and your brother take in a lot of dogs."

"A few," he said.

He gave me some instant coffee and, without mentioning any malamutes, told me about thirty or forty of the dogs, and then he took me out to see the ones he had then. The pens were a little crowded, but I could see that they'd been shoveled and swept recently, and only a few dogs had their ribs showing. One, I would swear, was a purebred Dalmatian. Roy talked the whole time. The image of the taciturn Yankee is something invented in New York City or Hollywood. The word *aye-yuh* is not.

"You ever get any Alaskan malamutes?" I asked when we'd resettled ourselves in the house.

"That crazy woman send you?" The crinkles reappeared.

"Who?"

"Lady drove me nearly crazy. A year ago it was, more. After an Al-ass-can mah-lah-mute." Margaret is not hard to imitate. "Called, then she showed up, but the dog was dead by then."

"A big, tall woman? Hair swirled up?"

"Aye-yuh."

As Roy told it, it was a long story. The dog had been hit by a car. Maine is, as the license plates say, Vacationland. People take their pets on vacation, and when the month's up, the pets that aren't standing by the door of the family station wagon get left on what the kids are told is a permanent vacation. "Fluffy had such a nice time that he didn't want to go home," Mommy and Daddy say. Sometimes Fluffy really has taken off for the woods. Sometimes Rover just pays a high price for not coming when he's called. For whatever reasons, when the tourists leave, too many Fluffys and Rovers stay. The lucky Rovers end up with Roy and Bud, who, it turns out, don't gas or shoot or drown them. Roy and Bud saw enough of that in Vietnam. They feed all the dogs and find homes for as many as they can.

As I listened to Roy, I felt ashamed of having thought the place wasn't classy enough for Rowdy. Instead of paint, shingles, and fence posts, these guys bought dog food. It may sound nuts, but I'll tell you anyway. I started to think that those rust spots on Roy's face were God's fingerprints.

"So she never actually saw the dog," I said.

"Dog was already dead. Gone. Lived two days and died. God almighty, did she get after me." He filled his cheeks with air and emptied them. "Did it have a white spot on its back? It did. How many dogs you see out there with white spots?" Actually, the dog in my Bronco had one, a withers spot, a patch of white on the withers, the highest part of a dog's back, above the forelegs. "And did it have a tattoo on its leg? We always check for a tattoo, you know. Ears and belly. I says to Bud, 'That big husky have anything on its leg?' 'Sure,' he says. 'Seen it myself.' "

"And? Did it?"

His face rolled itself up.

"You had a lot of dogs then," I said, smiling. "Do you really remember that one?"

His face unrolled. I hadn't meant to insult him.

"Pretty dog," he said. "Like a little wolf. A pretty blue-eyed wolf."

"You don't see that too often," I said. "A blue-eyed dog."

"Well, I seen it then," he said.

"Did the woman ask you about that? About the dog's eyes?"

"Asked me about the white mark. The tattoo."

"Did you tell her? About the eyes?"

"You can't tell that one nothing," he said.

He made me think of that corny Cambridge joke. You can always tell a Harvard man, but you can't tell him much.

As I drove back out toward Union, then past the fairgrounds, I thought about Margaret and the dog. Roy's woman had clearly been Margaret. It would have been just like her not to ask about the dog's eyes. "Alaskan malamute," she would have repeated, as if anyone would know exactly what that meant. She would have condescended and belittled, and she would have asked about the withers spot and the tattoo. Not all malamutes have a withers spot, and few have any tattoo at all. It would have been just like her not to bother asking about something that all malamutes share: brown eyes.

It made sense. King—or Rowdy—took off in Blue Hill. Someone's Siberian was hit by a car and taken in by Roy and Bud in Union. The Siberian died before Margaret saw him, and she almost certainly believed that King had died. King, meanwhile, made his way from Maine to Massachusetts. Malamutes aren't really sled dogs, but sledge dogs, bred to pull heavy loads for long distances. A dog like that with nothing to haul strolls effortlessly from Blue Hill, Maine, to Pepperell, Massachusetts. Why had he gone south? By chance? Maybe not. At that time of year, most of the traffic would have been from summer people heading south. One of the things I'd noticed about Rowdy was his tendency to follow anyone or anything moving fast. A malamute, like a wolf, wants to go where the rest of the pack is going, and at that time of year, the human pack was going south. He reached Pepperell, and while he was fixing a chicken dinner, a kindly guy interrupted him. The Siberian Rescue League picked him up and delivered him to Bobbi. She and Ronni gave him a shower and fed him well, and Bobbi didn't have to work too hard to talk Dr. Stanton into taking him. His instincts had taken him south, luck had got him to Bobbi, and once she had him, Dr. Stanton's love for dogs had taken him within half a mile of Margaret's house. It was a strange coincidence, but nothing more.

We didn't get to Cambridge until ten that night. Rowdy hadn't had much exercise for the past few days. Neither had I. In the morning, I put on my running shoes, and we set out down Concord Avenue toward Fresh Pond. November is too late for Indian summer and too early for "the January thaw." November doesn't have enough warm days strung together for anyone to have taken the trouble to name them. But it has a few, and this was one. In the bus shelter by the playground sat Hal Pace, eyes closed, not waiting for a bus. Just waiting. On the sidewalk in front of the armory, Gerry Pitts was raking up leaves, ice-cream wrappers, and discarded homework papers and depositing the debris in green plastic lawn-and-leaf bags. We said hello to each other. He was in his shirt sleeves. On his right forearm was a four-inch tattoo of a rococo anchor.

Chapter 12

GERRY and that anchor on his arm, the Navy, Margaret's dead brother, Margaret herself, Antarctica, Valium, Rowdy and his papers—I did a lot of thinking on that run. I decided I might be getting paranoid about the Navy and that I needed a healthy dose of reality. I also realized that if there was one person who should have recognized Dr. Stanton's Rowdy as Margaret's King, tattoo or no tattoo, it was Janet Switzer, his breeder. I had to meet her.

Running is supposed to build confidence. Maybe it had. I called Kevin at the Central Square station and told him I wanted some information and didn't want to tell him why. I asked him to find out when Dr. Stanton, Gerry Pitts, and Margaret's brother, Bill Lytton, had been in the Navy and where they'd been stationed. Either my postrunning confidence or Kevin's access to my nonvegetarian, nonteetotal kitchen convinced him. He promised to check.

The issues of the *Malamute Quarterly* I'd borrowed from Dr. Stanton's library were still in my kitchen. Toward the back of each was a page headed "Breeders' Directory." Snowcloud was listed between Snokimo and Southsongs:

> Snowcloud (pdsbh). 508 372-6586. Janet Switzer, 501 Greenwood Avenue, Bradford, MA 01830.

Bradford is a semirural section of Haverhill, an industrial city on the Merrimack River, about thirty-five miles north of here. According to the key to abbreviations, *pdsbh* meant puppies available, grown dogs occasionally for sale, stud service to appropriate bitches, dog boarding available, and a handler, too. There weren't any other abbreviations. Snowcloud did everything.

The same issue of the *MQ* had a couple of full-page ads for Janet's dogs. One of them showed a photo of "Am/Can Ch. Snowcloud Kotzebue Denali, C.D.X.," an American and Canadian champion in breed, a Companion Dog Excellent in obedience. Most of the dogs in most of the other ads in the *MQ* were standing posed at a show. In almost all of the ads, the dog faced left, and the handler's right hand was pulling up on the dog's collar to lift his head. The handler's left hand was busy making sure that the dog's tail was over his back and displayed to good advantage. Denali's picture was different from the others. Holding a perfect show pose without any human assistance, he stood alone in a snow-covered field. The text under the photo described him as the grand old man of Snowcloud. It claimed that he wanted to congratulate several of his children and grandchildren for some obedience titles and a grandson for a major win in breed. It was easy to see why Janet Switzer was proud of the dog. I felt proud, too. Rowdy looked just like him. Damn those papers.

Margaret had chosen the kennel well, one that produced what are called well-balanced dogs, breed championships before their names, obedience titles after. What's more, I was willing to bet that she'd picked that particular sire or grandsire, Denali.

Janet Switzer was home when I called. She agreed to an interview about the special challenges of training northern breeds. After she gave me directions, I told her that I had Dr. Stanton's malamute. In obedience, lots of people know lots of people, but the world of malamutes is tiny. I didn't want her to hear about Rowdy from someone else.

I have a cousin who lives in Haverhill, which used to be Shoe City, U.S.A. Although the Merrimack, which separates Haverhill from Bradford, has been somewhat cleaned up, the city still stinks like an old boot. Unemployment, alcoholism, small-time prostitution, and drugs have replaced the shoe industry. According to my cousin, Haverhill made a trade with Lyndon Johnson in the late sixties. The city gave him young men for Vietnam. In return, the War on Poverty bombed the center of Haverhill. That trade may sound bizarre, but the story must be true because there's a long list of names on the Veterans' Memorial, and the exact center of the city shows unmistakable signs of having been razed about twenty years ago.

I missed the Bradford exit from 495 and ended up driving through Haverhill, then over the bridge and through unblitzed Bradford, past the college, down Kingsbury Avenue onto Greenwood, and into farm country. A neatly lettered gray and white sign for Snowcloud hung from a post by Janet's driveway. Across the street was a cemetery. It was a good location for a kennel. If you raise dogs, the best neighbor is a dead neighbor.

Janet's house was a diminutive blue cottage with white shutters. In the drive stood a long tan RV, a tan house trailer, and a tan Chevy wagon. Inside the Chevy was a wagon barrier to keep the dogs in the back, and on its bumper was a trailer hitch. The collection of vehicles was typical for someone who does a lot of traveling to dog shows. Also typical were the bumper stickers all over the rear ends of all three vehicles: "Caution Show Dogs, Do Not Tailgate," with a drawing of a malamute. "Malamute Power." "I'd rather be driving sled dogs." "On the eighth day God created Alaskan malamutes."

No one answered the doorbell, so I walked to the side of the house and peered over the gate of a wooden fence. Inside was a professional setup consisting of a couple of sheds, several rows of chain link runs separated by gravel paths, and a stretch of rough lawn. Inside the runs were wooden platforms, upended tires, and doghouses, and above part of each run was a sheet of corrugated green plastic to give shade in the summer. From the top of a flat-roofed wooden doghouse in the run closest to me, Denali stared at me and led fifteen or twenty other malamutes in a chorus of their woo-wooing substitute for barking. He'd aged a little since the picture in the *Quarterly* was taken, and he could have used an hour's brushing, but he had a thicker coat than Rowdy's, the kind of coat that malamutes develop only if they live outdoors in the cold, and an alpha-wolf air of dominance.

"Hello?" I called out. "It's Holly Winter."

"That will do, thank you," a clear voice said authoritatively to the dogs. "Denny, that's enough. They like to pretend they're guard dogs. Holly Winter? You're Buck's daughter," she informed me.

Janet was older than I'd expected from hearing her high voice on the phone. Her short, curly brown hair was streaked with gray, and her face was weather-lined. She was hefty for someone who lived in a dainty cottage and in those miniature houses on wheels, and she wore rugged clothes, thick green corduroy pants, hiking boots, and a tan parka with tooth-shredded pockets. One of the ways she met the special challenges of training malamutes, I suspected, was to keep those pockets filled with bits of dried liver to reward the dogs. On the left shoulder of the parka was an embroidered patch with a picture of a dog and the words *Alaskan Malamute.* I fumbled with the handle on the gate, but she strode over and let me in.

"Your father tried to buy one of my dogs once," she said. "I didn't make the connection until after you hung up. That's one thing you get when you breed mals, you know, guys who want to use them for hybrids. I won't sell to them. And then you get the macho types who want a tough-looking dog to scare the neighbors. And I won't sell to them, either. If you want to know the truth, about one person in ten thousand deserves an Alaskan malamute, and my job's to spot the one person."

I've read that every now and then, an alpha female heads a wolf pack. Here was one. I was glad that I hadn't come to convince Janet to let me have one of her dogs. Janet was a little more outspoken than a lot of breeders, but her attitude wasn't unusual. Instead of trying to sell you a dog, a good breeder will evaluate you to see if you're good enough.

"This is Denali, isn't it? I saw his picture in the *Malamute Quarterly,*" I said as I walked over to the big dog's pen. "It seems to me that one person in a million deserves a dog like him."

A prize show dog is a prize show-off. Denali hurled himself from the roof of the doghouse to the cement of his pen, shook himself, loped over to the chain link, rose on his hind legs, and licked my face through the mesh. In what I think was an alpha-wolf test of a newcomer, Janet opened Denali's gate and let him out. According to the AKC standard, the Alaskan malamute is "playful on invitation, but generally impressive by his dignity after maturity." Never say that the AKC lacks a sense of humor. Denali ran up to me, sniffed my hands, legs, and feet, then flopped onto the ground to present me with his thickly furred tummy. I knelt down, rubbed, and told Denali how gorgeous he was.

I must have passed Janet's test. She introduced me to all the dogs. There were eighteen, ranging from Sassy, a nine-month-old bitch, to Leo, a twelve-year-old veteran of a research lab. He was a sweet old boy whose only sign of the years before his rescue was occasional drooling.

We visited the dogs, let them take turns running loose, and talked about training for at least an hour. Janet was no Margaret Robichaud. I'd been right about the liver.

"What you have to understand," Janet said, "is that malamutes are very intelligent. A lot of jerking on the collar just doesn't impress them. In fact, it's apt to make them decide you're stupid. You talk to them a lot, work out your relationship. You let them know you're the head of the pack, and, believe me, a lot of jerking on a collar won't convince an Alaskan malamute of anything except that you're a jerk yourself."

"You don't use training collars?"

"Oh, I use them. I've tried training halters, too, but they're all just signals," she said. "To a malamute, they're not punishment. They're not correction. They're just a reminder. So's food. A malamute understands that it's all a game, and reward's part of the game. Really, you don't obedience-train an Alaskan malamute. They don't really obey. They're not supposed to. They think with you. You want a dog that obeys you when you tell him to pull the sled onto thin ice? No, you want a dog who'll override you if you make a dumb decision. In so-called obedience, they do what you want because they like you and they want to please you, but it isn't obedience. It's cooperation. But you've got a malamute. You know all that, I hope."

"I've been given some expert instruction lately." I grinned. She knew I meant Rowdy.

"I've talked you nearly to death," Janet said. "Want some coffee?"

I did. Her kitchen was about the size you'd expect to find in the house trailer. Four 40-pound bags of ANF dog food were lined up along one wall together with a stack of metal feeding pails. On one wall was a poster with the word *Alaska* and a drawing of two wolves howling. When Janet took off the parka, I wasn't too surprised to see a blue T-shirt with an orange moon and a team of dogs pulling a sled across her heavy breasts. Janet turned on the gas under a battered kettle. She set the table for coffee, producing two mugs decorated with pictures of . . . guess what.

"I interviewed Margaret Robichaud a little while ago," I said.

"I should never, ever have sold her that dog," Janet said. "I knew it at the time, and I don't know why I did it. Well, I do know . . . but it was a bad reason." She sighed with regret. "You know who she is. That woman is a real power, and she knows everyone. How do you say no to someone like that? I tell her no, she can't have one of my dogs, and she talks to everyone, and I mean everyone, and eventually, the judges start looking funny at my dogs. So I told myself it was good for the dogs, good for the breed. I'd heard all about what she thought of malamutes, her remarks about temperament, and I was pretty tired of it. You know, that was a lovely puppy, one of Denny's, and I told myself, 'Well, if this one doesn't win her over, it can't be done.' What can I say?"

So Denali was the sire. "She never had anything bad to say about the puppy," I said. "She says she adored him. In fact, she says she didn't have the heart to get another malamute after she lost him."

"Fecal matter, that's what that is." Janet poured boiling water into the mugs.

"Are you sure?"

"Did she tell you all about how well her jerk on the collar worked with him? 'Minimal low-key praise. Make him understand that he has no choice about obeying. Minimal praise, maximal correction.' Right?" She leaned forward and pointed a finger at me.

"Yes," I said, drawing back.

"That's fecal matter. You know how I know? I've got eighteen dogs out there right now." She waved her hand toward the back window. "I've had Alaskan malamutes for thirty years. And let me tell you, you give any one of those dogs minimal praise, and what you'll get back is nothing, believe me. It just won't work. I know these dogs. My first husband tried that. He had German shepherds. I gave him one of my dogs, and before long, that dog started to turn mean. And I have never, never had temperament problems with my dogs. I just couldn't put up with that."

Like any other premium dry dog food, ANF provides a complete, balanced diet, but from the expression on Janet's face as she thought back on the incident, I fleetingly suspected she'd supplemented ANF by feeding her first husband to the dogs.

"I think you would have liked the way Frank Stanton was with his malamute," I said. "Rowdy, his name is. He's a sweetheart."

"Frank was a dear man," Janet said. "I used to see him all the time, at shows, you know, everywhere."

"He must have loved Denali."

"You know, the last time I saw Frank, I was showing Denny in Veterans. At Bayside."

Veterans is what's called a nonregular obedience class. It's for dogs eight or older. They have to have obedience titles. They don't gain any points toward anything. It's a way to keep them happy when they're too old for jumping but still active enough to enjoy performing.

"Did you ever see Rowdy?" I asked.

"Nope. Never did. If he wanted a mal, I don't know why he didn't come to me."

"He didn't decide to get a mal and then find Rowdy," I said. "It was the other way around. He saw Rowdy, and that's what decided him. He's a lovely dog, and I think Dr. Stanton didn't want to take on a puppy."

"Bring him out here sometime," she said. "Where's he from?"

"I don't know," I said. "I haven't got his papers yet."

"You're going to show him?"

"I hope so," I said.

"Of course you are," Janet said.

Just before I left, Janet asked me a strange question: "You heard anything funny about Margaret Robichaud lately?"

"Funny?"

"Yeah. I wondered."

"I don't think so," I said.

"Something happened that I thought was a little odd. A couple of months ago, it was. In Novice. One of her bitches fell asleep."

"In the ring?"

"On a down."

"I haven't heard about it," I said. "It is strange."

I felt sad when I left because I wished that I could have shown Rowdy to Janet. Denali was getting old, and she would have been thrilled to see a new Denali, young again. I also felt that I'd eliminated one person from my list. There was no doubt that Janet would have recognized Rowdy as one of her own, but she would never have threatened to take him from Dr. Stanton and would never have taken Dr. Stanton from him. If anything, Janet would have tried to prevent Margaret from getting Rowdy back. And, without a doubt, even if Janet had somehow managed to sneak into the armory during the fun match, she would never have tried to overdose any malamute.

Chapter 13

BARBARA Woodhouse wrote somewhere that a heaven without one's dogs would not be the heaven we hope for. Do you know who Barbara Woodhouse is? Who she *was*, I should say—she's now presumably in just that heaven she hoped for. Her TV series on dog training immortalized the word *walkies* and the phrase "Wha*t* a goo*d d*og," all spoken in her distinctive British voice. For a lot of people in Cambridge, Massachusetts, however, heaven is a particular place that does not allow dogs: the bar of an overpriced restaurant called Harvest. Harvest is in Brattle Square, around the corner from Harvard Square, near what Cambridge people call the old D.R. building. Design Research was a store that went out of business a long time ago, but Cambridge people still say D.R. the same way they still refer to the Harvard Square Theater as the U.T., even though it hasn't been the University Theater for decades. What they call the old D.R. building actually houses a store called Crate and Barrel, and it's really the *new* D.R. building. About twenty years ago, the Harvard Graduate School of Education tore down the original D.R. building to put up a library, something I happen to know because when I was little, Marissa used to take me to the *old* old D.R. to buy special Christmas ornaments and drops of amber and blue glass to hang in my bedroom windows, and every time I walk by the library, I remember those Christmas trips.

To return to the topic of heaven, the menu at Harvest is pretentious, and the food isn't always wonderful, but the bar is shabby and stylish, and everyone goes there, including tourists who hope to see someone famous like the president of Harvard or Robert B. Parker. Steve and I were at the bar in Harvest, but we hadn't seen anyone famous. We weren't looking. After a tiff about something I'd rather keep to myself, we hadn't seen much of each other lately. But we'd made up. Neither of us can even afford to drink at Harvest, so going there was a special treat. We'd both put on clothes that weren't dog-torn or cat-snagged, and we'd taken turns brushing fur off each other with one of those red velour lint removers. We looked pretty spiffy, for us.

"You're a vet. Tell me something," I said. "Why would a dog fall asleep on a long down?"

"Fatigue. Boredom."

"In the ring?"

"A mellow dog?"

"I don't think so," I said. "Doesn't it seem weird? I've seen dogs go to sleep in class, like at the end of the nine o'clock class, but at a show? In the ring?"

"It's possible," he said. "I'll bet it's happened."

"It has. One of Margaret's goldens did," I said. "Let's get another drink and talk about Valium."

We ordered refills. The drinks at Harvest are reasonably generous.

"Valium could sure make a dog sleepy. Look what it did to you," Steve said as he ran a hand through my hair.

"It didn't kill me," I said. "I thought I was dying, but they told me at the hospital that it's hard to kill yourself with it. One of the doctors said they get failed suicide attempts with it all the time. And the other thing she said was that the worst part isn't the overdose. It's coming off it. So what else? Medically."

"Valium, otherwise known as diazepam, is one of the most overprescribed drugs in the U.S., maybe in the world. It's a benzodiazepine. Do you want me to spell that for you?"

"No, smart ass," I said.

"Okay. One point is that it has a long, long half-life. You

take it at bedtime to go to sleep, and it's still in your system all the next day. Longer. Sometimes much longer. It's addictive. Contraindicated in pregnancy."

"And indicated when?"

"When someone has anxiety. Insomnia. Muscle spasms. Acute alcohol withdrawal. It's an anticonvulsant."

"And for dogs? Do you prescribe it?"

"Hardly ever. Sometimes for acute stress. Plane travel for nervous animals. Or suppose the owner's going crazy because the dog's agitated about something, I'll sedate the animal for a day or two. Like if the dog's crated near a bitch in season."

"Vicarious sedation," I said.

"Right. It can be a matter of safety. Like some cats go berserk in a car, even in a nice dark carrier, howl and shriek. Now, if I've got an owner who's moving to Chicago and has to drive there with a nervous cat, I'll sedate the cat. Otherwise, somewhere around Buffalo, the owner's going to have an accident or strangle the cat or throw it out the car window."

"So who's taken a trip with a nervous cat lately?"

"No one that I know of."

"Have you prescribed any Valium lately? Maybe you're not supposed to say."

"I'm telling you, I don't like Valium. I hardly ever use it. Just when it's needed. The big plus is that it doesn't decrease blood pressure, so I'll use it for older animals, a dog with a cardiac problem."

"You know who does use it?" I spoke softly. "On himself?"

"Who?"

"Vince. He left a jacket at my house, and when I checked the pockets to find out whose it was, I found a bottle."

"Forget it."

"Why?"

"That was for back spasms, just a temporary thing. He told me about it."

"Where was he when I was in the ring?"

"Watching. So was Ron."

"No," I said. "Ron was outside, patrolling."

"Not then."

"Are you sure?"

"Absolutely. We talked about it later, how well you'd done. Look, what would he know about that thermos?"

"He'd know it was mine. So would anyone else. It's got 'Winter' written on it in big letters on adhesive tape. And my parka was on top of it. Ron does know I carry the thermos a lot, I guess. Last spring he and I did some obedience run-throughs for that group in Brookline, and I used to take it. For Vinnie. I was worried she wasn't getting enough water, you know, for her kidneys. So he's seen it. But he's no murderer. Besides, he likes me."

"Everyone loves you, Holly. Someone just thought you'd be more mellow with a little Valium in your system."

"You have a point there."

"Look," he said. "We're both going to have more brandy, and then we're going to think about this systematically." He signaled for another round.

"Means, motive, opportunity," Steve said when the drinks arrived.

"Right."

"Let's consider Stanton's murder first. Means? Strength. Is there anyone we can eliminate?"

"We're all strong," I said. "Except Millie, I guess."

"Who's Millie?"

"His housekeeper. If you want to think about motive, she had one, I guess, only she didn't, really. She's been with him for ages, and they were friends. But she's about four feet high and frail. She really couldn't have done it."

"Let's forget motive for the moment. Who had the opportunity? Who was outside?"

"Or," I said, "who wasn't inside?"

"Right."

"Ron, maybe," I said reluctantly. "Remember? He was in the men's room."

"He said he was in the men's room."

"Gerry could've been out there," I suggested.

"No, he couldn't," Steve replied.

"How do you know?"

"I saw him, that's how."

"Are you positive?"

"Yes. What about that homeless guy?"

"Hal," I said. "And Margaret. Avon Hill's what? A ten-minute walk from the armory? Fifteen minutes? And talk about motive."

"Stop! Slow down! We're still on opportunity. We need some more brandy."

We had more.

"Then there's Roger Singer," I said. "He could have arrived there early. He's built like a gorilla. Can I talk about motive yet?"

"Sure."

"Motive. Money," I said.

"He gets hardly any."

"Maybe he was greedy. Maybe he just hated his uncle. Maybe all of those boring Sunday dinners drove him into a mad frenzy."

"Murders do usually take place in families," Steve said.

"That's usually husbands and wives, isn't it? Stanton was only his uncle. Great-uncle, actually. You don't see many headlines like that in the *Globe.* 'Man Kills Great-Uncle.' "

"Motive," Steve said, ignoring me. "You want motive? Ron Coughlin. That guy has a practically pathological identification with the club. Look at the old *cui bono:* Who gains from Stanton's death? The obvious answer is the Cambridge Dog Training Club."

"Ron knows he isn't the club," I said. "Sure he identifies with it. I do, too, sort of. But he's not crazy."

"Then there's that guy Hal," Steve said. "Could he have had some irrational motive?"

"Kevin thinks he didn't have anything to do with it. And

who couldn't have some irrational motive? I could. You could."

"We had no opportunity," Steve said. "Remember, we're being systematic."

"You want to know who has everything? Margaret," I said, probably a little thickly.

"You don't like her, do you?"

"She hates my father, and she owns my dog."

"Your father has nothing to do with this, Holly."

"Fine," I said. "We'll talk about Margaret. We don't know that she wasn't there."

"That's systematic," he said. "And how about you and Rowdy?"

"We didn't do it," I said. "Rowdy wouldn't kill anyone."

Steve exhaled and rolled his eyes. "I'm talking about the overdose. Means?"

"Vince had the means," I said.

"No," Steve said. "He was only on Valium for a couple of weeks, some minute dose. There's no way he had enough."

"Okay. Forget Vince," I said. "Who else had Valium?"

"That's something else we don't know."

"Margaret," I said, "has been doping her dogs. I just know it. And let's talk about blackmail."

"Blackmail isn't the right word."

"Extortion. Whatever. Whatever Dr. Stanton was paying, because Kevin says he was paying, and it was enough so he was hurting for money."

"Okay. I agree. And I agree that it must have had something to do with the dog, because that's what he cared about. That's what he'd have paid for."

"Exactly," I said, but I think it didn't come out quite like that. "Janet Switzer's out. She'd have known in one second that Rowdy was one of her dogs, and I'm sure she'd have known he was the one she sold to Margaret. But, first of all, I don't think she ever saw him with Dr. Stanton. And, second, I really think she'd have paid to let him stay with Dr. Stanton."

"Bobbi what's her name?"

"Reed. I don't think she made the connection, though I could be wrong. And I don't think Ronni did, either. Bobbi just isn't the kind of person who wouldn't tell me. And, look, they've spent a lot of money on their place, but I'm pretty sure that Bobbi has money from somewhere, and Ronni makes a lot. They did call him King, but so what? Anyway, I could swear that Bobbi believes that Margaret's King died. But that's the thing I don't get about Margaret. I mean, on the one hand, I'm almost positive she thinks that King died."

"Or she used to think he'd died," Steve said.

"Yes. In fact, I know that. On the other hand, she's suddenly got all this money. She's really campaigning those dogs. And would she ever have loved to watch Stanton squirm! Plus, I know you think my idea about Antarctica is crazy, but it could be a powerful motive for someone. Suppose her brother was the commander of that ship. She's a twisted enough character herself. Maybe her brother was, too, in a different way. And suppose Stanton knew or found out. And she wouldn't just be out to protect her brother's memory, would she? Though that could've been a big part of it. Buck says she adored him. The other part is, it would rub off on her, wouldn't it? I can't see her sailing into a show with everyone knowing that her brother was the one who nearly exterminated a breed. She'd die first . . . or kill."

"Okay, maybe Stanton, just maybe, but what about you? She had no opportunity. None. She was not at the match. She was not in the armory. Practically everyone else was. She wasn't. You just don't like her. And if she was going to strangle Stanton, she'd have done it a couple of years ago. Why now?"

"He had something on her," I said. "Her brother. Dope. Something. He knew she was doping her dogs, and he was going to report her to the AKC."

"Big deal."

"It would be for her, believe me."

"You're guessing."

"Yes," I said. "But someone was paying her something. Or is paying her. You should see those kennels. And the dogs. She's been taking them everywhere."

"Speaking of taking people places," he said, "we should take ourselves home. If we can."

Fortunately, we hadn't driven to Harvest. The cold November air had a sobering effect. As we walked up Brattle Street past the Harvard Graduate School of Education and the Loeb and the Longfellow house, Steve held my hand and tried to persuade me that I was growing paranoid about the Navy and Margaret and that I should come clean with Margaret about Rowdy and then take my chances. He thought she might even give or sell Rowdy to me.

"That's impossible," I said. "You don't know her."

"What about seeing a lawyer? A court might decide that he's not hers. She hasn't been in possession for over a year. Get an ILP number. You hate handling in breed anyway."

"But I don't hate owning a champion in breed," I said. "Besides . . ."

"Besides?"

Some things are almost too embarrassing to admit, even to Steve. "I know who he is. For an ILP, I'd have to lie to the AKC." In case you haven't guessed, that's a mortal sin.

"I think we need more information before I do anything," I said as I unlocked my back door. "You know what I want you to do?"

"There's nothing I wouldn't do for you." He smiled. "Tell me everything."

I did.

If I had a theme song, it wouldn't be "Show Some Emotion," but that doesn't mean I don't care about him. He's a great vet and an even better man.

Chapter 14

THE next morning, after three aspirin apiece, Steve and I embarked on our systematic program. We started with Hal Pace because we thought he might know something he hadn't told the police and we thought it was worth finding out whether he'd tell us. The Cambridge police are used to guys like Hal, but guys like Hal are also used to being hassled by the police. My hunch was that as Hal had sobered up, he'd shut up in the hope of getting back on the street as fast as possible. We put Rowdy in the back of the Bronco—India was at Steve's clinic—and drove around to scan Hal's favorite spots. When Rowdy caught sight of an Australian shepherd running with a young couple on Memorial Drive, he roared and yelped so wildly that my head pounded. Otherwise, he wasn't too bad.

We found Hal on Ware Street, which runs from Harvard Street to Broadway. He was dragging a big clear-plastic bag full of cans and bottles. I knew he was headed for the Broadway Supermarket, one of his favorite places to cash in his finds. We parked the Bronco in the supermarket lot across from the store and waited for Hal outside.

"Hi, Hal," I said when he came out. "Remember me? Holly Winter? From the armory?"

Hal must have had his colors done at the Society of St. Vincent de Paul. He had on a green down vest, a baby-blue plaid flannel shirt, baggy maroon pants, and brown work boots with crimson socks, but his clothes were cleaner than usual, and he'd shaved within the last two or three days. As always, those angles and planes in his face triggered the fantasy that he was the lost heir to some fortune or throne, but his clumsiness spoiled the image. He shuffled back and forth, examined the sidewalk, and studied the sky.

"I'd like you to meet my friend Steve Delaney," I said. "Steve's a vet. He takes care of my dog. You like dogs, don't you?"

He nodded.

"I've got my dog with me, in my car. You want to say hello to him?"

I didn't wait for an answer, but set off across the street in the hope that Hal would follow. Steve took the cue and walked with me, and so did Hal. I unlocked the back of the Bronco, opened its gate, took Rowdy's leash, and let him jump out. As always, he was bouncing and smiling, eager to ingratiate himself with everyone.

"Don't touch the dog," Hal said.

"It's okay," I said. "He likes to be patted."

I made a show of running my hands up and down Rowdy's back. He must have thought he'd done something wonderful.

"See? He likes it."

Hal mumbled something.

"What?" I asked.

"Don't touch the dog," he said again.

"Hal, did someone tell you that? Not to touch the dog?" Steve asked gently. "This dog doesn't bite. You can pat him."

Steve joined in my little demonstration of the safety of patting Rowdy.

"You know this dog, don't you?" I said. "You used to see him at the armory. With an old man. He was the old man's dog, the man who died."

Hal pulled his shoulders into an exaggerated shrug, stretched his neck out, tilted his chin up, and rolled his head back and forth.

"That was a bad night," I said. "Everyone was scared. And you had a really hard time."

He quit the head rolls and, for once, looked at me.

"We know you didn't do anything bad," I said. "We know

you didn't hurt the old man. But we want to find out what happened, and we want you to help."

I knew I was moving too fast, but I was sure that if I slowed down, he'd wander off or run away and we'd lose him altogether.

"Hal," Steve said, "we want you to come to the armory and show us what you saw. Just us. You and me and Holly and Rowdy. No police."

"No police," Hal said suspiciously.

One of the problems with trying to talk to Hal was total uncertainty about what he understood. For all I knew, we could have used ten-syllable words without losing him, but something about his expression made me keep it simple.

"Right," I agreed. "No police."

"We're all going for a ride," Steve said, "and then we'll take you wherever you want. It won't take long."

On the way to the armory, Steve talked quietly to Hal about dogs and cats, about being a vet. He invited Hal to visit his clinic. Hal didn't say much, but I had the feeling that he understood the invitation. I parked beyond the armory, in front of the playground, close to the rain shelter where people wait for the Concord Avenue bus.

The playground is really half park and half playground, with slides and a wooden climbing structure and jumping contraptions and also trees, paths, and benches. At that time, it was more of a blend than usual because the old fences had been torn down a few months earlier, and the new ones hadn't yet been installed. As a result, there was no barrier between the playground and the paths and benches, as well as no barrier between the playground and the baseball field that stretches along Concord Avenue and back to the Tobin School. It was fortunate in more ways than one that the city's renovation hadn't been total. Fresh fir bark had been spread around the bases of the maples, but the trees themselves hadn't been touched. They didn't need rejuvenation. They're thicker and taller than saplings, but still healthy young trees, and they hadn't needed replacement or pruning.

All of us, including Rowdy, got out of the Bronco, and Hal headed directly down the right-hand side of the playground until he came to a heavily branched tree. He paused and looked expectantly at Rowdy, who stopped sniffing the fir bark and obligingly lifted his leg on the designated maple.

Hal gave a gleeful laugh that actually sounded like "Ha-ha-ha-ha-ha," and I knew immediately, in some way that I can't explain, that his pleasure wasn't scatological. It was more primitive than that. What he liked was seeing something predictable, familiar.

"Is that his favorite tree?" I asked, and Hal repeated the ha-ha routine.

"I bet Dr. Stanton used to walk him here," Steve said. "Before class."

The city of Cambridge doesn't encourage people to walk dogs in the playground. In fact, there's a fine for it. One reason is something called toxocariasis, which is caused by a parasite that can spread from dog feces to people and, in particular, to children's eyes, where it causes severe damage, as Dr. Stanton would, of course, have known. He'd also have known that Rowdy didn't have toxocariasis, so maybe he'd considered Rowdy exempt. Furthermore, before the recent improvements, there were no lights in the playground and few streetlights on Concord Avenue, and behind the park was the unlighted playing field, then, in the distance, the Tobin School. It was as dark as a city ever gets. He could have been almost certain that he and Rowdy wouldn't be caught. Still, it seemed peculiar that an ophthalmologist would have flouted a law, even a minor one, meant to protect children's eyes.

"The old man used to bring Rowdy here?" I asked. "To this tree?"

Hal nodded.

"You used to talk to him? Did you talk to the old man?"

Hal's eyes moved to the left and right as if he were thinking about taking off.

"Did he know you were here?"

Hal shook his head left and right.

"You were in the playground," Steve said softly. "It's okay. Show me where you were."

Hal looked a little nervous, but he walked toward the playground equipment and pointed to a boxlike part of the wooden climbing structure. Of course. This must be one of his thousand hidey-holes.

"We need to know everything that happened, Hal," Steve said. "Everything. The night the old man died. You remember that night. Show me everything that happened, and then we can go visit my dogs and cats. You can help feed them if you want."

That did it.

"You were here," said Steve, pointing to Hal's refuge in the climbing structure. "The old man walked Rowdy in. This dog. And the dog went to the tree, the tree you showed us. Was anyone else there?"

Hal shook his head left and right. "Don't touch the dog," he said.

"It's okay to touch this dog," I said. "He's a good dog. He doesn't bite. Do you want to hold his leash? Take his leash, and show us what the old man did."

Somewhat to my surprise, it worked. I held out Rowdy's leash, and Hal took it. Rowdy pulled on his end of the leash, and Hal trailed after him back to the big maple. Rowdy sniffed what was probably his own mark on the base of the trunk, and Hal reached up and stuck his hand in the lowest fork of the tree.

"All the time," Hal said with a broad, empty smile.

"He always did that?" I asked.

"All the time," Hal repeated.

Steve and I looked at one another.

"He put something there? Took something?" I said.

"He left something," Steve said. "And then, later, someone always came and got it, right, Hal? A man or a woman?"

Hal pushed his shoulders backward and twisted his mouth.

"A woman," I said, "with a yellow dog."

"A man," Hal said so loudly that I jumped.

"Do you know the man?" I asked. I knew it was a useless question, and I was surprised that he answered at all.

"Nice big dog," he said, and his face took on a guilty expression. He said exactly what I anticipated he'd say, not to touch the dog, and I saw a bit of what had happened. I didn't know when it had happened, but I could see it.

"Some dogs like to be patted," I said, "like Rowdy." Hal still had his leash, and I leaned over and again demonstrated enthusiastic patting. Rowdy sat down, leaned against me, and gave me one of his gentle-wolf stares. He was going to remember this day forever. "There was a big dog here, wasn't there? And you touched the dog. You patted the dog. It's okay. We won't tell anyone. Was it Rowdy? Was it this dog?"

Hal shook his head.

"A big dog?" I asked. "Bigger than Rowdy?"

There aren't too many dogs much bigger than Rowdy.

"Big dog, nice big dog." His tone of voice was the one everyone uses to talk to dogs. Rowdy liked it. He stood up and fixed his eyes on Hal.

"You talked to the dog," I said. "And you patted it. Where was the dog?"

He looked puzzled.

Steve understood. "Right here. Here, by this tree. And the man let you pat the dog?"

Hal bent down and wrapped Rowdy's leash around the trunk of the tree.

"I get it," I said. "The dog was tied to the tree. The man tied the dog to the tree. Then the man left. And while he was gone, you patted the dog and talked to it."

Hal's was the sly grin of someone who's gotten away with something.

"Don't touch the dog," he said with self-satisfaction.

I dropped Steve and Hal at the clinic, went home, took more aspirin, and slept for three hours. At four, after a shower, coffee, and deep meditation on the pros and cons of drinking brandy, I called Steve.

"Did he say anything after I left?"

"Just guess."

"Not to touch the dog. Anything else?"

"Not a thing."

"So what do we know now? We know he patted a dog," I said.

"We know a lot," Steve said. He has the kindest voice I've ever heard. "The branch of the tree. That's where Stanton left his payments. 'All the time,' remember? Thursday was someone's payday. Before class, Stanton would leave an envelope in the fork of the tree."

"I get something now. You know, at first, it didn't make sense that he'd walk his dog in the playground. An ophthalmologist, of all people, you know? If anyone should be in favor of keeping dogs out of playgrounds, it's an ophthalmologist, especially an ophthalmologist who loves dogs. I mean, suppose some kid in Cambridge gets toxocariasis? The place is anti-dog enough already. So Dr. Stanton would, first of all, be in favor of the law, and second, he wouldn't want to stir up trouble by having people complain about a dog in the playground. So he didn't decide to go there. He was acting on orders."

"And the big dog," Steve said. "The one Hal patted. I wish we could tell for sure when that happened. I also wish we could tell who picked up those payments. Anyway, I've got a feeling that big-dog episode was a one-shot deal, and I'll bet it was the night Stanton died."

"I wonder if he'd recognize the dog."

"Or the man."

"He'd be great in court."

"The ideal witness," Steve said. "But I did check something out. I went through our records here, at least for everyone at the club who's a client, everyone I could think of."

"And?"

"And Dr. Draper was a lot freer with Valium than I am."

"And?"

"I've got a couple of things. Last spring, Roger Singer's Newfoundland developed something that looked like eczema plus some wheezing, maybe asthma. Draper checked out the usual things, and then he put her on prednisone, which didn't help, and she had a bad reaction to it. He tried antihistamines and did some more tests and kept her under observation, but he still didn't find anything. At that point, she was starting to do herself some damage from scratching, and she had bad perivulvar dermatitis. He put her on Valium. I might not have done it, but it seems to have worked."

"Roger."

"Second, Vixen. When Ron brought her in for her shots last December, he also got some Valium because he was taking her on a plane, but it was hardly any."

"He went to San Francisco, I think. California, anyway," I said. "He has relatives there. Okay. Obviously, a Newfoundland is the classic big dog. Lion is a lot bigger than Rowdy. Vixen? What do you think?"

"She's tall," he said. "She's leggier than Rowdy. He's bulkier. Also, his fur's so thick."

"I don't think you look at her and think 'big dog.' And why would Ron tie her up? You wouldn't need to. You'd just tell her to stay. But you'd have to tie Lion up. Concord Avenue's right there. And what does Lion weigh? A hundred and thirty pounds? More? Roger must have got a ton of Valium."

"Draper's good. He's experienced," Steve said. "But he did overprescribe. Singer had enough for you and Rowdy, too. You know, though, maybe someone else did, too. We see a lot of dogs, but we don't see them all."

"So who didn't have Valium? Or who didn't get it from Dr. Draper?"

"Roz. Vince. Ray and Lynne. Diane. Arlene. You."

"Me?"

"We're being systematic."

"Margaret?"

"She's not a client of ours."

"So who does she see? Can you find out?"

"I can try," he said. "But I can't promise anything."

Kevin knocked at the back door a few minutes after I hung up. I still didn't tell him about the tattoo. I did tell him about Roger, and he in turn put my mind to rest about Ron.

"Coughlin was repairing a pipe. There's no way he could've been there," Kevin said. "And he's explained that visit to the can. To my satisfaction."

"How?"

"He had the runs," Kevin mumbled. You'd think a cop could talk frankly about bodily functions. The man obviously needed another dog. "He made four trips that night, at least."

"Are you sure?"

"Couple of people saw him leave and come back. Guy even had his doctor call."

Kevin had some other information, too. Neither Dr. Stanton nor Gerry Pitts had served in the Antarctic. Bill Lytton, Margaret's brother, had.

I also pried out of him the news about Hal Pace, but it was no news to me.

"They say he's got a thing about dogs."

"You know what that means? He likes dogs so much that he keeps talking about them. He talks about them so much that they think he's brain-damaged. They'd say the same thing about me."

"Some of us already have," Kevin said.

When he finally left, I called Buck to tell him about Bill Lytton, mostly because Steve wouldn't take it seriously and Buck would. He takes anything seriously if it has to do with dogs. I was hoping that he'd have some idea of how to follow it up, too, but all he did was tell me again about Bill Lytton's famous hunting dog.

"I heard that one of Margaret Robichaud's dogs fell asleep in the ring," I told him. "On a long down. Have you heard anything about that?"

"I've heard," he said. "Lots of people have heard."

After I hung up, I realized that I didn't know where Rowdy was. I found him in my bedroom. I'd forgotten to close one of the drawers under the bed. Carefully distributed over the comforter, the floor, and the windowsills were all the socks I own, every clean pair, at least. Rowdy hadn't chewed or torn them. He'd just arranged them for me. Smug and proud, ears up, eyes bright, tail twitching, he was sitting in the middle of the room waiting to enjoy my reaction.

"Cute," I said appreciatively. "Now, if you're such a smarty, put them back."

I had a big grin on my face. A dog doesn't pull a trick like that on a stranger. He doesn't do it to you unless he wants to make sure he's your dog.

Chapter 15

IT took me all day to turn my scrawled interviews with Bobbi and Margaret into articles. Rowdy spent most of the time asleep in the bedroom. Every hour or so, he'd wander into the study, scratch my jeans with one of his front paws, give me an imploring look, whinny at me, and rest his head on my lap. After dinner, I put on my navy parka, gloves, and a watchman's cap, leashed Rowdy, and started out for a walk.

I don't understand how a woman can live in a city without a big dog. If you're afraid to go out alone after dark, don't just complain about violence and oppression. Want to take back the night? Get a dog, and not a pocket poodle. The second you get that big dog, the world will become an infinitely more polite place than it was the second before. Get a mixed breed, a crossbreed, a Rottweiler, a German shepherd, an Airedale, a Doberman, a Newfoundland, a Bernese mountain dog, a Rhodesian Ridgeback. Get an Akita. Someday I will. With a well-trained Akita at your side, you could walk coolly through Hell.

As a special treat for Rowdy, we followed Concord Avenue to Garden Street and wandered around Harvard Square. Rowdy loved Harvard Square. It's busy and smelly. In the square, we ran into some people I know, and we spent some time talking with them. I had lots of compliments on my husky. Someone mistook him for a German shepherd. We headed up Mass. Ave. to Porter Square and took Walden Street back to Concord Avenue. It must have been about nine-fifteen when we got to the corner of Appleton Street, or, as it's correctly pronounced in Cambridge, the cawnuh of Appleton and Concud.

Dog lovers who believe in ESP would tell you that while we were roaming through the square or looking in shop windows on Mass. Ave., Rowdy should suddenly have plunked himself down, tilted his head toward the moon, emitted a series of howls, and torn off in the direction of that cawnuh. At the very least, they would say, his hackles should have gone up as we passed the Lyn Hovey stained-glass shop on the corner of Appleton and Concord, and when we crossed Appleton and walked by the funny little building that occupies the edge of my property and forms one wall of my yard—it's called a spite building, why I'm not sure—a precognitive fit of growling and snarling should have seized him. Maybe he has no sixth sense. He padded up Concord Avenue, lifted his leg on a corner of the spite building, and wagged his plumy white tail all the way up the steps and through the hall to the kitchen door, which was ajar.

If I'd had all my ordinary senses and brain cells functioning right, I'd have remembered that my next-door neighbor is a cop, and I'd have taken my chances with Mrs. Dennehy. I'd have kept Rowdy's leash in my hand. What I did was turn on the kitchen light switch, let Rowdy loose, and walk in as usual. Everything looked normal except for the kitchen door, which was ripped up and had its lock broken, and the open door to my study. I always, always keep that door shut except when I'm actually in my study. Rowdy did not growl, check the place for intruders, or stand protectively at my side. He ambled over to his water dish and lapped. I grabbed his collar and pulled him with me to the study. My worst fear about a robber or a rapist or a mugger isn't what he'll do to me or my house. My worst fear has always been that some sick bastard will hurt my dog.

There was no one in the study to hurt either of us. Nothing was there that hadn't been there before, but most of what was there was on the floor. The entire contents of three metal filing cabinets, the contents of all six drawers. File folders. Paper. Diskettes. Books. The bricks and boards that had been bookshelves. The computer, thank God, was still on the table, but the printer had been knocked off its stand. Your brain doesn't operate right at a time like that. Instead of wondering whether someone was in my bedroom or living room, I thought about the printer. I toyed with the idea of lifting it back onto its stand and starting it up. My heart was beating hard, but I wasn't crying or shaking. What brought me to my senses was the sound of Rowdy's claws digging into the diskettes, probably ruining any that weren't already hopelessly scratched. I leashed him and edged slowly out.

When I knocked on the Dennehys' back door, I still had that false calm a crisis gives you. Mrs. Dennehy came to the door.

"Is Kevin home?" I asked as clearly and politely as if I'd been giving foreign students a lesson in English as a second language.

Kevin was home, and he took charge. He called his buddies, got his gun, refused to let me go home, and placed me in the care of his mother, who installed me at her kitchen table and dosed me, not with scotch or brandy or Valium, but with sweet, milky herbal tea. Cops are exempt from the Harvard no-wallpaper ordinance. Mrs. Dennehy's kitchen is papered in a pattern of yellow teapots and blue bunnies on a tan background. I'd never noticed the bunnies before. They made me nervous. Mrs. Dennehy always makes me nervous. Instead of fastening her gray hair into a bun in the usual way, she must drive the hairpins into her skull with a hammer. She always looks as if she's stoically suppressing pain. I started to shake, and she gave me more herbal tea and patted me on the back. To calm myself, I did what I've done for as long as I can remember. I clung to my dog, buried my face in his fur, and breathed in that scent of domesticated wolf.

Kevin returned before too long and took me home. By then, I wasn't shaking. I was furious. In my study and bedroom, a couple of detectives were dusting for fingerprints. Their gray powder was all over the doors. It was probably all over my diskettes, too. I answered a lot of questions. No, nothing was missing, not that I could see. Papers, maybe. Diskettes.

After powdering the living room door and poking around, Kevin's buddies gave us permission to use the living room. We sat at opposite ends of the couch, oddly formal, as if we were about to sip Harvey's Bristol Cream and munch on petits fours without dropping any crumbs. Although I'd twisted the valve on the radiator to give us some heat, none had yet arrived, and the old ashes in the fireplace made the room smell even colder than it was. Rowdy sat in front of me and kept offering me his paw.

"I'll tell you one thing," Kevin said. "This is no professional job. You've got a tape deck in here, camera in plain sight. Another thing. First thing a professional does, he makes sure he's got a way out. He makes himself a bolt hole, opens a window, breaks the lock on another door, anything. This guy didn't. I don't like that. Professional, you don't need to worry. Guy comes in, makes sure he can get out, picks up what he wants, leaves. He's in and out in a couple of minutes. You're the last thing he wants to see. This guy was after something. Papers?"

"Maybe he was desperate for information on electronic flea collars," I said. "He just couldn't wait for *Dog's Life* to hit the stands."

Kevin didn't smile. He held up what looked like a Ziploc bag. "The guy left you a present."

"A plastic bag?"

"The bag," he said, "is ours."

"Oh, an evidence bag. Is that right?"

"Containing one large clump of fur. Color, yellow. You didn't, uh, keep any?" He sounded suitably embarrassed.

"I don't save dog fur. I weave not, neither do I spin." Mrs. Dennehy must have put me in a biblical frame of mind. Some people, of course, do save the fur when they groom their dogs. One of the books I'd borrowed from Dr. Stanton's library had a picture of hats and mittens knitted from malamute fur. I'd just as soon crochet my own hair.

"You didn't have some as a kind of, uh, memento?"

"Of Vinnie? Of course not. If I want mementos, I've got pictures and ribbons and trophies. Did you think I gave her a haircut after she died? What kind of creepy idea is that? Where did you find that stuff?"

I once knew a woman who did something even creepier. When her dog died, she took its body to a taxidermist. The stuffed dog sat forever on its favorite chair in her living room. The dog was, or had been, a smooth-haired fox terrier. The woman was French. I asked her whether this kind of thing was customary in France, but she said no, it was unusual there, too.

"The fur was on your bed," Kevin said. "Right on top of the bed."

"What's that supposed to mean?"

"A calling card. A message to someone. You. Me."

"That's freakish," I said. "This guy is some kind of pervert. Burglars don't take their dogs to work. Was there a dog here? Can those guys tell?"

"They haven't finished yet, but they think no," Kevin said. "They think no dog. Just fur."

"A coat without a dog. Like a grin without a cat," I said. "Like the Cheshire cat." I didn't like the idea of that fur on my bed.

"What kind of dog would you say this came from?"

He handed me the plastic bag. I got up and held it under the light from my standing lamp.

"It's like Vinnie's," I said. "A golden retriever. Some dog with a coat like a golden's."

"Sit down," Kevin said. "You and I need to have a little discussion. We received a piece of correspondence today. Unsigned. The gist of which is to suggest that if we want to know who murdered Stanton, we should start by taking a close look at his dog."

"Oh?" I said innocently.

"Well?"

"Well, go ahead," I offered. "He won't bite. Or do you want me to call a vet?"

"I want you to tell me what the hell is going on."

"I'm glad your mother can't hear you," I said. "If you yell any louder, she will."

"I'm telling you it's time to stop playing games. Some weirdo has trashed your house and dumped dog fur on your bed. The same weirdo nearly overdosed you. An old man died. You saw him? Did he look pretty? You eager to get your face done like that, too, Holly?"

"No," I said quietly. If I hadn't adopted Rowdy on the night Dr. Stanton died, I'd have thought a lot about that face. In fact, I'd have taken everything seriously, but when there's a dog around, especially a dog like Rowdy, I find it hard to be scared.

"What all this has in common is dogs," Kevin said. "And for some reason, when I think dogs, I think you."

"I haven't done anything," I said.

"Right. Now you start. Talk to me about that dog. Now."

Kevin didn't frighten or intimidate me into talking. He startled me. I'd never heard him sound like that before. Besides, once he'd decided to look closely at Rowdy, it was inevitable that he'd find the tattoo.

"What he's got is a tattoo," I said. "It's an AKC registration number. He belongs to Margaret Robichaud."

"Good girl," Kevin said.

"Don't patronize me, you bastard. I'm telling you everything."

"I'm glad my mother can't hear you," he said.

We both laughed. Rowdy walked over to Kevin and offered his paw. Kevin took it.

"I'm telling you everything," I said, "on the condition that I keep this dog. He's not going back to her."

"Homicide and animal control have recently merged into

one department," Kevin said, "but I'll make an exception in your case."

I spilled everything, including the rumors about Margaret drugging her dogs and my suspicions about her brother.

"So," I wound up, "Margaret hated Stanton. And even if she originally thought that King died, she could have seen him around here. Avon Hill's close enough to Brattle and Appleton, and Stanton walked Rowdy. She could've put two and two together. And if she did, she'd just have loved tormenting him. Plus, she could have had her revenge without taking Rowdy, her King, back. And you missed something big."

"I did, huh?"

"Money," I said. "When you looked in her backyard, you didn't know what you were seeing. She's got the most incredible kennel I've ever seen, and I bet you didn't go inside it. How much was Dr. Stanton paying out?"

"Two thousand a month," Kevin said.

"For how long?"

"Eight months or so."

Sixteen thousand, tax free. I wasn't sure it was enough to have financed that setup, but I didn't say so. Maybe she'd counted on more coming in. I wondered where she'd been earlier that evening. Out walking her dogs?

What I didn't wonder was whether to shake the remaining fur off my comforter and curl up in my own bed that night. I guess I could have nailed the kitchen door shut and toughed it out, but I didn't. Sleep wouldn't have come easily with my livelihood lying in a crushed mess on the floor of the next room. Steve and I live separate lives, but that night, I didn't even call before I showed up at his place with Rowdy at my left side and a small suitcase in my right hand. Steve lives over the clinic, and I can't usually go to sleep there unless we run the white-noise machine to mask the barking, but that night I made him put the machine on low, and I persuaded him to station India right outside the bedroom door. A strong man next to you in bed is a comfort, but real security is a German shepherd bitch on guard at the door.

Chapter 16

Rowdy wasn't a big help with the cleanup. To him the roar of the vacuum cleaner was the growl of a mastiff. Dust mops were invading Shih Tzus. Sponges were rodent prey to be shaken until their necks broke.

The printer did work. The books had been scattered but not torn. Refiling wasn't much fun, but all of my important papers seemed to be there. The only irreparable damage was to the diskettes. Someone must have had it in for them. Some had been bent, and most had been ground underfoot. Fortunately, I'd kept hard copy of most of the files, and I'd stashed some backup diskettes in my bedroom closet.

Kevin's cousin Michael showed up to repair the torn wood on the kitchen door and install dead-bolt locks on the front and back doors. As I cleaned and filed and reassembled the bricks and boards and listened to Michael singing—like so many Cambridge carpenters, he also plays in a band—I thought about guard dogs, and I thought about that fur on my comforter. When a dog deposits excretion, he's marking his turf with a message for the next dog to come along. I've been here, he's saying, so watch out. Or maybe, I thought, I've spent too much time around dogs.

I also thought about Akitas and German shepherds and, you may be surprised to hear, golden retrievers. Hunting dogs won't necessarily guard a house, but they will guard you and your family. And what about the dog I already had? A few days earlier, he'd accidentally run into me while we were playing Frisbee. If you want to know what it feels like to be hit by an Alaskan malamute going full speed, sprint into a brick wall. Would he use that power? Would he bite? His teeth and jaws were smaller than Clyde's, but you needed to examine the dog and the wolf dog side by side, jaw by jaw, to notice the difference. If Rowdy perceived someone as a threat to me, he could metamorphose into a speeding, wolf-jawed brick wall. But would he? If a dog attacked him, he'd unhesitatingly ram into it, slash its ears, and crush its muzzle. But a person? Attacking me? Did he have it in him to see a human being as a threat? On my side was his alert intelligence; on the other side, his gentle disposition, his apparently universal trust that people were put on earth to rub the tummies of Alaskan malamutes.

I called Buck to fill him in and to make sure that no one alarmed him with a misleading account of my burglary. Not burglary. Why did I keep calling it that? Nothing was missing. *Breaking and entering* were the right words, but I didn't want to think them. My house has been robbed, I could say. It's been ransacked. I've had a burglary. But someone "broke in"? Someone "entered"? *I'd* been broken and entered. That's how I felt.

"What do you think about an Akita?" I asked my father.

It was a stupid question. Mention any breed of dog, and Buck thinks it's terrific. Ask whether you should get a dog, and he thinks it's an inspired idea.

"Interesting breed," he said. "Helen Keller had one."

"I was thinking of a guard dog," I said, "not a guide dog."

"Oh, hers wasn't a guide dog. It was a pet. What do you want with a guard dog? What happened to the Smith & Wesson? Where's your .22?"

In his own way, he's quite protective. He gave me the Smith & Wesson for Christmas last year. The .22 was a present for my fourth birthday. They're both in the closet of my bedroom in Owls Head with the double-barreled shotgun and the deer rifle and a couple of Buck's other birthday and Christmas presents, but I didn't say so. He gets his feelings hurt more easily than you might think.

"I can't carry a gun through Harvard Square," I said. "And I didn't ask you about a gun. I asked what you thought about an Akita."

"Great idea," he said.

Rita tells me that parental consistency and predictability are important for children's mental health. How nice for me. I got Buck off dogs and guns without getting him started on wolves or fishing by asking whether he'd heard any more about Margaret Robichaud. He'd been making some subtle inquiries about Margaret, or so he said. Subtle he's not. A couple of people had told him the story about the dog that fell asleep in the ring. According to one of his sources, Buck said, everyone had been surprised because the golden was a young one, not some jaded veteran.

"The kind of dog you might want to calm down," I said. "You'd just want to shave off that nervous edge."

"You bet," he said.

I'd invited Steve for dinner, and since I had to cook liver that day anyway, I made some for us. Liver is nutritious. I hate it, but I try to be practical and efficient. Any pet supply house will sell you dried liver, but compared to the liver you cook yourself, it's pretty unappealing. It's against the rules even to carry food into the obedience ring, but I like to use liver as a reward during training. Some people don't believe in edible rewards. Their kitchens probably smell better than mine. To cook liver for dogs, I take beef liver slices and roast them slowly, uncovered, until they're almost completely dry. After the liver has cooled off, I cut it into little pieces and freeze it. I fried Steve's and mine with butter and onions.

Over the liver and onions, Steve told me that he'd run into a classmate from veterinary school, Lisa Blumenthal, who has a practice in Belmont. I know Lisa. Her husband, Don, raises goldens. Steve had mentioned Margaret to her, and Lisa had been eager, he said, to make a confession and also to complain. Margaret had taken her goldens to Lisa for their heartworm tests, and while she was there had pressed Lisa for something to calm them down on the road. Lisa, of course, knew who Margaret was.

"It wasn't that Margaret said anything outright," Steve told me. "But Lisa got the message, namely, that a few words from Margaret wouldn't help Lisa's reputation, or Don's, either. So Lisa gave in, and guess what Margaret left with."

"Why did Lisa give in like that? She must have felt awful. Didn't she think she was practicing bad medicine?"

"Not exactly. She felt weak but also protective about Don. Afterward, she was sorry she'd done it, but it was too late."

"You know," I said, "I can imagine Margaret dumping Valium in my thermos."

"Pouring," he said. "It must have been dissolved first."

"Pouring it. I don't know how she could have got to the thermos, but it's something you can see her doing. And I think she could strangle someone, especially Stanton. But breaking in here? And that business with the fur."

"There's something weird about that," he said.

I agreed.

Thursday, of course, means dog training. We left both cars in my driveway and walked the dogs to the armory. The young off-duty cop the club had hired was lounging inside the door talking to Gerry Pitts and John, the manager of the shelter. The cold must have driven the cop in. It was four below zero, so bitter that even Rowdy was glad to get indoors. Malamutes can live outdoors year round, regardless of the cold, but only if they're acclimated. To tolerate subzero weather, they need to build up their coats. A house dog adapts to inside temperatures, and he's as comfortable outdoors at four below as you are.

Vince's advanced beginners were working on the figure eight. They had a long way to go. Every dog there was lagging on the outside loop. At the far end, Roz's Utility group was doing scent discrimination. Steve and I had moved so fast in the cold that we were early for our eight-thirty class with Roz, so after we checked in at the desk with Barbara Doyle and Ron Coughlin, we hung around there. Barbara had only one shepherd with her, Freda, who was stretched out on the floor. Vixen was sitting at Ron's side, impatient to get to work. I ran my hands over her. Her coat was only a little like a golden's, paler and shorter. And Ron? He looked like what he was, a nice guy in a good mood, an ordinary guy, a capable plumber, a gifted handler, nothing more.

And Ron's good mood? His conversation with Barbara and Steve left no doubt that he was enjoying the prospect of Dr. Stanton's legacy. They were speculating about what the club would, or rather could, do with the house at the posh end of Appleton Street. The capriciousness of Cambridge zoning combines with the eccentricity of Cambridge people to mean that you can never tell what will and won't be allowed here. One thing we wouldn't be able to do was hold our classes there. The house didn't have a room even half big enough. It wasn't clear whether we'd be able to use the house as a library or, as Barbara was suggesting, a library and museum.

"If you ask me," I said, "the real problem is going to be parking. It's permit only, and the neighbors aren't going to want a lot of new permits issued, and they're also not going to want us to turn half the yard into a parking lot."

"We wouldn't need many permits," Barbara said. "How many people are going to be there at once? Not many more than when Frank was alive. It's not as if we wanted to open up a shop."

"We'd want to meet there," Ron said. "That'd be, what? Six or eight cars?"

"People have that many now," I said. "Shrinks with offices in their houses. They have therapy groups that big."

"Not the same thing," Ron said. "That's not official. The shrinks live there. The neighbors put up with it. What about a parking lot? It wouldn't have to be big. A long, wide driveway."

"I'll bet it depends on how they feel about dogs," Barbara said. "If that block has a lot of dog lovers and they back us, it'll go through fine. If we've got dog haters, we haven't got a chance."

"Plus," Steve said, "it'll be a public building. We'll need fire escapes, fire doors, inspections of the electrical system, plumbing."

Ron rocked back in his chair and grinned. "I guess I can tell you about the last time I inspected the plumbing," he said.

"What's wrong with it?" Barbara asked.

"Nothing now. This happened last spring. March maybe."

"The pipes froze," I said.

"Too late in the year for that. It was skunk weather."

We all laughed, mainly, I think, because having a skunk spray your dog is the ultimate unfunny event. It goes on being unfunny for a long time. Unlikely as it might seem, Cambridge has skunks and raccoons. They live on garbage.

"Here's what happened," Ron said. "Frank's away. Millie's on vacation. He leaves Singer to house-sit and dog-sit."

"When he got that award," I said. He'd been inducted into some ophthalmological hall of fame. "Whatever it was. He was really excited about it. Remember?"

"He was," Barbara said.

"So," Ron continued, "I get a call from Singer. This is maybe Wednesday, and his uncle's due home Saturday. He tells me the bathtub drain's clogged, and I show up, and the tub's full of water and fur, and the drain's full, and I mean full, of fur. So I open it up and I ask him what's going on, and he tells me Rowdy got loose and a skunk got him, so he's been trying everything to kill the smell so his uncle doesn't find out he's let the dog loose. And Rowdy's shedding."

"Wella Balsam," Barbara said. "And tomato juice."

Ron laughed. "Right. There's tomato juice all over the walls. Looks like a slaughterhouse. And he's poured on vinegar, and there's a drugstore's worth of shampoo bottles around, and he's begging me not to tell his uncle. He's like a great big kid. You should've heard him. 'I said I wouldn't let him loose,' he says to me. 'Don't tell my uncle.' "

"The big baby," Barbara said. "It was probably just an accident."

"Dr. Stanton didn't like accidents," I said. "Did he have both dogs there? Lion, too? Where was Lion when all this was going on?"

"Sick," Ron said. "In the hospital."

"When she lost all that fur," Barbara said. "What was it? Eczema?"

"Probably," Steve said. Lion was Dr. Draper's patient then, not his. He hadn't even been in Cambridge, but no one asked how he knew.

"I wonder if Dr. Stanton ever found out," I said.

"Not from me he didn't," Ron said.

From eight-thirty to nine, we worked with Roz on Pre-Open. Rowdy was a born jumper. He'd sail over the broad jump or the high jump and plant himself right in front of me. The smug expression on his face said that he knew how good he was. Unfortunately, he'd also discovered a new trick with the dumbbell, tossing it around in his mouth when he should have been holding it steadily in his closed jaws. He thought the tossing act was cute, but no judge would agree.

At nine, after we helped Roz put away the broad-jump hurdles and the high jump and finished folding up the mats—you need them for jumps to keep the dogs from slipping on the floor—all of us joined Vince for our regular Novice class. Roger had shown up with Lion, who was at his left side in that sloppy, crooked sit Vince had been telling him to correct. We lined up, handlers and dogs, along the wall. I followed an impulse to stay away from Roger, but I heard Ron, who was next to him, laughing, and when I looked down the line of people and dogs, I could see Roger's red face. Now that Dr. Stanton was beyond caring about whether Rowdy had been loose, Ron obviously felt free to rag Roger about the skunk and the bathtub. Ron was grinning and gesturing, and

I was pretty sure that Roger was hearing how funny we'd all thought the story was.

I found it less hilarious than Ron did. Every bath that Roger had given Rowdy was a chance to see the tattoo, and he could have called the AKC. How many baths had it been? Five? Ten? More? Hadn't he told me that he'd never bathed Rowdy? I wondered how he'd managed to get Rowdy into the tub so many times. With all my experience, I'd had to use a muzzle, but Roger had a size advantage. He probably outweighed me by eighty pounds. He wouldn't have had to push and pull as I'd done. He could have lifted Rowdy. With those thoughts came a memory of something trivial, something I'd forgotten. Last year, in the late winter or the early spring, Roger had a cast on one arm. He'd said something about slipping on the ice. It happens all the time here, and I hadn't thought any more about it. Rowdy was sitting squarely at my left side, his mammoth front paws, for once, even with my feet, the way they're supposed to be. For once, he was looking up at me, watching for a signal to move. Gentle, happy, eager to work, this was a dog I wouldn't have wanted to lift unmuzzled into a bathtub even if I'd had the strength. I'd have been afraid of being bitten. I'd have been afraid of having my arm broken.

"Let's see some nice straight sits," Vince said. "You lose points for a crooked sit, you know. Handlers, forward. Nice loose leads."

There's a book to be written on Zen and the art of dog training. Training requires total concentration. If you're not all there, neither is your dog. If you're jumpy, so is your dog. For the next hour, my mind was where it belonged, on Rowdy and Vince and straight sits and a loose lead. When I noticed Roger at all, it was only to notice what a lousy handler he was, careless, inattentive, and inconsistent. He'd even put the wrong size training collar on Lion, inches too long, and his lead was a heavy one with a big snap. When the lead was loose, the extra chain hung down, the weight of the chain and snap tightening the collar. That's incorrect, of course.

When you jerk on the lead, the collar should tighten, then instantly loosen again.

At the end of the nine o'clock class, everyone was tired, and Gerry and John were eager to have us clear out. I put on my parka, zipped it up, pulled on my gloves and hat—new, blue with a row of sled dogs, a present from Steve—and grabbed my purse. In a gesture of defiance, I'd left it under my parka, as usual. Let someone steal it. Let someone plant a bomb in it. The armory was, after all, my church, and I wasn't going to desecrate it by acting paranoid.

Steve, India, Rowdy, and I left the hall with Roger and Lion ahead of us. The entryway was crowded with men keeping warm as they waited for the shelter to open. By then, the temperature outside must have been six or eight below. Hal was squatting on the floor near the doors to the outside. As I started to move toward him with one of those hello smiles forming on my face, Lion shook herself playfully, and Hal sprang upright and bolted out of the building, out into that six or eight below.

"He'll come back," John said. "He always does."

I hoped so.

Chapter 17

JUST as I shot back the new dead bolt on the door, the phone rang. The call was from Steve's answering service, an emergency message about an Afghan hound hit by a car. While Steve talked to the owners, I listened to the warm rumble of his voice. If your dog is ever hit by a car, that's the voice you'll want to hear, but better not to let it happen. Cars are only one threat to a loose dog. The word *dog-napping* sounds silly, but dog-napping is no joke, and the guy who steals your dog isn't necessarily looking for a pet. Research laboratories pay for dogs, and some laboratories don't ask many questions. Some don't ask any. What happens to Rover in the lab? No one wants to think about that.

Steve didn't deliver any diatribes to the owners of the Afghan hound. As long as the owners aren't abusing the dog or telling Steve to put a healthy dog to sleep because they're too lazy to train it, Steve is usually understanding about pet owners' occasional lapses. He arranged to meet the Afghan and its owners at the clinic and rushed off. If he weren't my lover, he'd still be my vet.

And if he were my lover but not a vet, or if he were a less conscientious vet than he is, I'd have stayed home that night, but dead bolts or no dead bolts, dog or no dog, the house felt empty and cold. It *was* cold. I'd turned the thermostat down to fifty-five when we left for dog training, and the old radiators are slow to heat up. I should have put on a flannel nightie and climbed under my comforter, but the comforter reminded me of that clump of fur, and the fur reminded me of Margaret and, especially, of Roger Singer. If Steve had stayed, we'd have talked about them, and I wouldn't have wondered where they were. With Steve and India in the house, I wouldn't have listened to the wind batting the leafless trees on Appleton Street or thought about the spite building on the corner of Concord and Appleton, my corner. It used to be a sandalmaker's shop, but Cambridge is a city where you wear boots, not sandals, for six months of the year. The narrow building had stood vacant since the sandalmaker closed shop. Was it locked tightly? It was unheated, I was almost sure, but it would offer shelter from the wind, shelter to wait for my lights to go out, or shelter for Hal while he drank up or worked up the courage to give the armory another try. I could almost see someone huddled in the spite building or crouched under the landing at my back door or flattened on the sand of the playground to wait for Hal. I've made some connections, I thought, but it isn't too late to shut me up before I find some hard evidence.

Hard evidence. The fur? That was more like soft evidence. If I could convince Kevin to search, he might find out exactly where it had come from, but what real evidence did I have? An old memory, a tattoo, an appointment book, ground-up diskettes, a veterinary prescription for Valium, the prickle of my skin. I knew too little to convince Kevin, and I knew both too much and too little to go to sleep.

My L.L. Bean Maine warden's parka is navy blue because I like navy blue, even though it shows dog hair. I didn't buy it because navy's an effective camouflage on a dark night, but right now I was glad it was. From one of the drawers under my bed, I pulled out a full set of pink silk long johns. I removed my jeans and sweater, stepped into the long johns, and put my everyday camouflage back on: the jeans and my black sweater, navy wool socks, dark brown boots, and my navy parka and gloves. I didn't wear the sled dog hat, but a black watchman's cap, and I stuffed my hair into it. I could have been almost anyone.

There was no disguising Rowdy, but I couldn't leave him

home alone. That he might have bitten Roger once meant nothing. If I'd tossed Rowdy into a tub too many times, he'd have bitten me, too, but he wouldn't have held a grudge against me any more than he held a grudge against Roger. If I'd put a training collar high on his neck and jerked and jerked and never praised, the way Margaret must have done, he'd just have decided I was a jerk myself. The next time I patted him, he'd have been all smiles and bounce, just as he was at the sight of my parka and gloves and his leash in my hands.

I switched on the outside flood that illuminates the driveway at the back of my house, held the key to the Bronco ready in my hand, eased open the back door, and surveyed the scene. Three or four kids, students, I guessed, were walking up my side of Appleton Street toward Concord Avenue, and I timed my dash to the Bronco so that they passed the end of my driveway as I unlocked the door, hurried Rowdy in, jumped into the driver's seat, and relocked the door. It took me a minute to convince Rowdy that the rules hadn't changed. I'd let him in through the front of the Bronco, not the tailgate, but he still had to ride in the rear. The Bronco felt like a cryogenics vault. I let the engine warm up for a minute, then headed for Avon Hill. The lights were on in the yellow farmhouse. I slowed up in front, then drove off. Through the golden curtains of the den, the inimitable Margaret was visible, striding across the room.

My next destination was Washington Street, Roger's apartment. I had no intention of knocking on Roger's door, but I was hoping that there'd be a light on and a moving shadow visible inside or some other sign to assure me that he was within his own black-furred white walls.

The Bronco is fairly distinctive. It's a shiny metallic blue, and it's so big that the car wash charges me a truck rate for it. I parked on Mass. Ave. in Central Square, near the Main Street fork and a couple of blocks from Washington Street. Anyone who saw the Bronco might think that Steve and I had gone to one of the clubs in Central Square, and I could always say that I was heading for one of the Indian or Chinese restaurants nearby. Even though you can wear anything anywhere in Cambridge, I wasn't exactly dressed for a jazz club. Rowdy would be harder to explain, but I couldn't face those dark streets alone. I counted on him to scare off most people, and he did. At the corner of Columbia, which leads to Washington, a pair of tough teenage punks underdressed for the weather passed us, and if I'd been alone, I'd have expected and probably been given a hard time.

"Hey, is that a wolf?" one of them called out.

"Yes," I said.

"Jesus," said the other kid.

They went on their way like little gents.

The cold was so intense that the wind burned the skin on my face and made my nose drip. I pulled my hood up and almost ran down Columbia and around the corner of Washington toward Roger's building. The lights were on in his front window, but no shadows were visible because he hadn't pulled the curtains or lowered the blinds. Since the apartment was on the ground floor, I could stand in the freezing darkness on the sidewalk and see in the window just as if I'd been at one of the drive-in movies we used to go to when I was in high school, except, of course, that the drive-ins closed in the winter and on raw Maine summer nights, we ran the heaters in the cars.

Roger's movie was about to become one of the X-rated Grade-C ones the drive-ins started showing a few years before they all went out of business. A bottle of wine and two glasses stood on the coffee table, just as they had when I'd been there, and the girl was standing, too, a skinny teenager with spiked green and white hair. She was so pale that her skin matched her hair. She wore black pants, maybe leather, and her shirt was off. Maybe she hadn't been wearing a bra to begin with. Her shoulders were thrown back, and she held her hands behind her as if they were tied. Maybe they were. Roger was kneeling in front of her, and as I was about to leave—I'd seen enough, thanks—he got up and moved toward the window. I was almost sure he hadn't seen me, and there'd been nothing to hear, but maybe he'd sensed a presence outside. He pulled the curtains. The girl was maybe fifteen, probably younger, possibly much younger.

At that point, I did hear something, the sound of voices, footsteps, and a door, the door of Roger's building as it opened to emit a man, a woman, and a dog. Rowdy hit the end of his leash so fast that he nearly pulled it from my hand. The temptation to go for another dog was something I hadn't been able to teach him to resist. I snapped myself back to a normal state of consciousness and tried to look like a person out walking a dog in eight below, not a sleazy Peeping Tom. I managed to yank Rowdy in the direction of Central Square. The couple with the dog walked in back of us. We passed under a streetlight, and a moment later, I heard the woman's high-pitched voice with its Harvard accent.

"His damn fur is all over my jacket." Her tone announced her as someone entitled to pass through life unfurred. "Why's he shedding now? Aren't they supposed to get a winter coat?"

"Could be hormones," the man said. "I'll take him in Monday."

"Maybe it's fleas," she said. "That place is a fleabag."

"Fine," said the man. "You find us another place that allows dogs."

"It's your dog," she said. "Christ, it must be twenty below here."

We reached Central Square, and I unlocked the tailgate of the Bronco. As Rowdy jumped in, I glanced at the couple, who'd caught up with us and were now quarreling their way along Mass. Ave. The dog was a golden retriever, a shedding golden retriever that lived in Roger's building. I selfishly hoped that the man was right, that the dog had a hormone imbalance and not fleas. If the woman was right, flea eggs were hatching on my comforter.

After Roger's freezing drive-in, the wholesomeness of my house was even more comforting than the warmth. I'd left the thermostat at seventy, and I turned it down to sixty, not my usual forty-five, for the night. I put on a flannel nightgown and I kept my long johns on under it, not because I needed the extra heat but because I didn't want to see another naked or half-naked body that night, even my own.

"It's child prostitution," I said to Kevin the next morning. I'd caught him on his way out to work, and we were drinking coffee in my kitchen. Mrs. Dennehy doesn't believe in caffeine. "Can't you get him on that?"

"You know," he said, "you're what they call naive. Here's what happens. He walks up to Central Square and picks up a kid who's got two choices. She stays out on the street, or she goes with him. It's cold on the street. She goes with him, and she's not cold."

"For Christ's sake, Kevin, you are not listening to me. He had access to the fur, and he's not just weird, he's weird in a sexual way. You know what I think about the fur? On my bed? I was wrong about it. It means my hair. That's what color it was. It means me."

"One, this city's full of weird people. Two, we pull in every guy that picks up a hooker, we got an empty city."

"There'd be women left," I said. "And girls. Teenage girls."

"With no way to support their habits and no place to get in out of the cold."

"There are shelters. Look, at least find out if she's all right. I shouldn't have just gone off and left her there."

"She's long gone."

"You don't give a damn, do you?"

"Look, Holly. I was busy last night. A twelve-year-old kid got shot in front of the courthouse. He's dead. You know who shot him? His mother. Maybe we've pulled her in by now. Maybe we haven't. If we have, that's what I do today. I have a nice chat with her about blowing her kid's guts all over the street."

"I know it's bad," I said.

"You don't know. You haven't got a clue."

"I know who strangled Frank Stanton," I said. "And I know who overdosed Rowdy and me. And I know who broke in here. And you won't do a damn thing about it."

"You *know,*" he said. "That's what you've got. You just *know.* You saw something you didn't like. Guy picks up a hooker. She's a kid. It isn't nice. You're shocked. He's a monster. Next thing, he's a murderer. It all follows, right? That's what you've got."

"So what have *you* got?"

"You. Wandering the streets feeling sorry for guys like Pace," he said.

"Not him again."

"The original weirdo. With a thing about dogs. I tell you that, and I get this liberal crap."

"Of course he's got a thing about dogs, but mostly he's just retarded, I think. And scared and confused. Do you seriously think he wrote that anonymous letter you got? He probably can't write at all. And I suppose he has a thing about diskettes, too? He knew to grind mine up because he knows what they are? He knows they're worth something? You know who'd go for them? A guy who sells software, and in case you don't know, that's what Roger Singer does."

"So do a lot of other guys. In the daytime, they push software. At night, they pick up girls."

"The night Dr. Stanton died, he could have been there early. He left his dog in the playground. Hal patted the dog."

"Right."

"It is right. Roger's big enough, and he could've got as close to Stanton as he wanted. Roger walks up, and what does Stanton see? His nephew. That's all. And the night of the match, he was there, and last year, he had enough Valium to put me to sleep forever. You know how big a Newfoundland is? He had Valium for her for months. Dr. Draper wrote big prescriptions. What if she didn't need all of it? And the night of the match, if he'd taken a look at Rowdy, he'd have seen a dog that had just had a bath, and he'd know that meant that I'd seen the tattoo. And that I'd call the AKC and find out what he had found out himself—that Rowdy was Margaret's dog."

"Did he know that?"

"Of course he did."

"They told you that."

"Not yet," I said. "They will. I'm sure they told Roger what they told my father, that Stanton's dog was Margaret Robichaud's, and that was all Roger needed. He's tired of waiting for Stanton's money, and puts the pressure on, and Stanton pays up. And I know where. He left it in the tree in the playground. Every Thursday night. Hal saw him."

"Funny. I didn't hear him say that. Did you?"

"Not in so many words, but that's what he meant."

"That's what he meant."

"Steve was there. We both saw it," I said.

"You saw a guy stand under a tree."

"Look, once Roger saw I'd given Rowdy a bath, he knew I'd make the connection, and first, he tried to shut me up, and it didn't work. Then he tried to capitalize on it. He decided to point the finger at Margaret, so he wrote that letter, and he left that fur here. But I think there's more to the fur than that."

"Fur? The charming Mrs. Robichaud happens to have four dogs with fur that matches your pretty hair. It *was* dog fur on your bed, you know. Did I tell you that? And the lab had something else to say about it. The dog had fleas."

"Margaret's dogs don't have fleas."

"All dogs have fleas."

"They all pick them up. But they don't all keep them. You can bet Margaret sprays her dogs after every show, just the way I do."

"Like I said, Holly, you're naive. And you're a pretty woman. It's a dangerous combination. I don't want you out at night. I know you; you're a country kid. This city is filled with guys like Pace."

"I'm not stupid."

"So you wander around alone at night, and then you tell me you're not stupid, right?"

"Right."

"Do yourself a favor. Stay home. Lock your doors. You think Pace is a nice guy. You feel sorry for him. You used to have it in for Robichaud. Now you feel sorry for her, right? And now you've got it in for the nephew. You don't know much, but you know what you like, huh?"

"Get going. You're late for work," I said.

"Take care of yourself. I'm serious."

"Don't worry about me. Worry about Hal Pace. He's no murderer. If I'm not the next victim, he is, and he doesn't have any dead-bolt locks because he hasn't got a door. He's out on the street now, and you can bet Roger Singer will be, too. He saw Hal run away just the way I did."

Chapter 18

THE woman who answered the AKC's phone had never heard of Buck Winter or *Dog's Life.* She was from a temp agency. She probably thought *chow* was nothing more than an army word for food. Mr. Chevigny wasn't in, she said. He had the flu. It had knocked out most of the regular staff at the New York office. Could she take a message? Better yet, could I write a letter? Requests to the AKC were best addressed in writing.

Mine weren't, but when I called Buck, Regina Barnes answered. Although I half expected her to tell me that requests to my father were best addressed in writing, too, she sounded less cranky than usual and promised to have him call me when he got back from Eastport. Eastport is on the Maine coast not far south of the Canadian border. It's had a badly needed economic revival in the last few years thanks to the Japanese craving for sea urchin eggs. Having exhausted the sea urchin supply in their own waters, the Japanese have turned to Washington County, Maine, the sunrise country, the easternmost part of the United States, real Down East. The inhabitants won't even eat mussels—they only recently started eating clams—but they don't mind evening the balance of trade. I knew what he was doing in Eastport. He's on a council that's supposed to promote friendly relations between Maine and Japan, and I was willing to bet that he was talking to some Tokyo business executive about Akitas and Japanese spaniels and cross-questioning him about why the Japanese are importing so many Alaskan malamutes. In a tiny country with a limited supply of meat for people, let alone dogs, a malamute must be the canine equivalent of a gas-guzzling stretch limo, but some malamute breeders are having yellow-peril hysterics about what the Japanese are doing with our dogs. Maybe the ghosts of the Malemutes are having hysterics about what *we're* doing with their dogs. If they ever catch us blow-drying them, they may materialize and demand them back.

Bonnie DeSouza, my editor at *Dog's Life,* is used to inexplicable underlining that turns out to be dog hairs, and apparent shifts from print to braille where someone overdue for a forepaw nail trimming has checked my copy, but the printouts of my articles about Bobbi and Margaret, retrieved from the floor after the break-in, looked as if they had been used for paper-training. The two articles were on a backup diskette, so I reprinted them both, and I read up on dog halters for the next column. There was a good article on halters in one of the issues of the *Malamute Quarterly* that I still hadn't returned to Dr. Stanton's library. Dog halters are a new fad. You use them in place of training collars. I filled out order forms and wrote out checks for four different halters.

I also ordered a harness for Rowdy, size 4XL, red, from a little company in Vergennes, Vermont, called Konari Outfitters. In the loft of Buck's barn was an extra sled he once accepted in exchange for a pup. Buck hardly ever used the sled he already had, so I don't know why he took a second one, especially because he doesn't really like mushing. The winter activity he likes is a hair-raising sport called skijoring. Harness the dog, wrap a special belt around your waist, run a line from the dog's harness to your belt, put on your cross-country skis, and off you go. Don't try it unless you're a great skier (Buck isn't) with a well-trained sled dog (Clyde isn't). Buck has no sense of balance. Luckily, Clyde doesn't like to pull, so they haven't yet had a serious accident. Clyde is, of course, a wolf dog, not a sled dog, but his wolf blood isn't what holds him back. Most people think that all Siberians, Samoyeds, and malamutes know how to pull and that other dogs don't and can't learn, but it isn't true. Dogs from incredibly unlikely breeds can be trained to pull—there's a guy who's done the Iditarod (Anchorage to Nome, about a thousand miles) with a team of poodles—and northern breeds aren't born knowing what *gee* and *haw* mean. Even so, if you're offered a dogsled and the choice of either a poodle or a malamute to haul it, take the malamute.

At four in the afternoon, when it was still light out, I walked Rowdy to Huron Drug, which is a combination drugstore and post office, to mail the halter and harness orders and the two articles. The temperature had warmed to a comparatively balmy twenty-five, and the slate-blue clouds that foretell snow were moving in. I had Rowdy heel all the way home, and he did well, at least for him. At the corner of Huron and Appleton, he spotted a Great Dane across the street. His ears and hackles went up, and I could see that he wanted to bolt, but he stayed where he belonged instead of lunging and jumping. When we got home, I should have worked on getting him to hold the dumbbell without tossing it, but I didn't feel motivated. He wouldn't need the exercise until Open, and without his papers, I wouldn't even be able to enter him in Novice.

I had dinner with Rita. We enjoy each other's company and have a lot in common, even though her ten-year-old dachshund has yet to attend his first obedience class. When she first moved in, I told her about the Cambridge Dog Training Club, but she said that Groucho was an obedience virgin and she liked him that way. He doesn't destroy the apartment and he's remarkably quiet for a dachshund, so I haven't pressed her. I asked her why anyone would want an untrained dog, and she said that as a therapist, she spends all day trying to get people to change, and when she comes home, she wants to find a creature she doesn't have to persuade to be any different from the way he already is. Rita and Mr. Rogers.

I considered asking Rita whether I could spend the night in her spare room, but avoiding my own apartment felt cowardly, and the dogs would have been a problem. Except for an occasional exchange of growls, Rowdy and Groucho were tolerating life in the same house, but asking old Groucho to welcome Rowdy would have been overstepping the limits, and I didn't want to leave Rowdy alone in my place all night.

By nine, Rowdy and I were back home alone. Steve was at a conference in Philadelphia. I called Buck, but he still wasn't home, and Regina snapped at me. I wondered what she was still doing there. I hoped she hadn't moved in. A stepmother might be tolerable, but not Regina Barnes.

I wandered around and tried to read, but Hal was on my mind. If I'd paid attention to Kevin, who is not always wrong, I'd have phoned John or Gerry to ask whether Hal had checked in at the shelter, but I felt restless. In truth, Kevin's order to stay in and lock my doors had given me wanderlust. Besides, the wandering I lusted for was nothing more than a quick walk to the armory to check on Hal. Nothing keeps me from dog training, and I'm not the kind of person who takes a car to go a few blocks. If it had been Thursday instead of Friday, I told myself, I wouldn't have hesitated and I wouldn't have taken the Bronco. What's more, I thought, Roger, once bitten, might be shy. Margaret didn't worry me at all. There was a golden retriever specialty show on Long Island the next day, and I assumed she'd already checked herself into a Holiday Inn and tucked herself into a king-size bed. And Hal? I saw him only as the threatened, not the threat. In any case, I'd stay near home, and I'd be careful.

According to Rita, rationalization is a better defense than denial. I'm not sure I can tell the difference. It seems to me that I took two slices of rationalization, slathered them with rebelliousness, sandwiched in a layer of denial, and bit in. Rita would say that my defenses were primitive. She'd be right. If you have the privilege of choosing your defenses, forget that Freudian gobbledygook. Get a Smith & Wesson and a dog. That's acting out, I can hear Rita say. At least it's acting.

The afternoon's slate-blue clouds hadn't lied. Heavy clumps of snow were sheeting straight down in the windless night. Less than an inch had accumulated, but the thin cover was enough to awaken Rowdy's ancestral memory. At the bottom of the back stairs, he froze in recognition, then raised his hindquarters and thrust his nose to ground, a doggy Proust nuzzling arctic madeleines. By the time he'd pranced and dashed his way to the corner of Appleton and Concord, God's own coat enhancer had given him a Best in Show sheen that no cosmetic spray would ever duplicate, and his joy had blunted my vigilance. The tags on his collar jingled like sleigh bells.

I'd been concentrating so hard on admiring Rowdy, keeping my grip on his lead, and avoiding his rocketing leaps and plunges that I hadn't checked under the back steps or peered into the spite building. Not until we reached the corner of Walden Street did I remember to run my eyes up and down the whitened roads and sidewalks and scan the black shadows for human forms. Cars passed by on Concord Avenue, their tires writing black lines on its snow-covered surface. From a house on the opposite side of Concord Avenue, not far beyond the Cambridge Alternative Power Company (solar panels and wood stoves), old rock blared, a movie sound track. (Whoops. Sorry about that. In Cambridge, one says "film.") I sang under my breath.

As the song said, the night had come, and the land was dark. Still, I could see ahead of us the back of a bulky, hatless figure moving, like Rowdy and me, toward the armory. Rowdy was not pleased at my silent tugs on his lead, but if I'd allowed him his usual hydrant, tree, fence, and hedge stops, the figure would have outdistanced us. As it was, within a block I recognized the figure, alone, dogless, lumbering along. Moments earlier I'd been singing brave words about not being afraid, but I was afraid. I had no one to stand by me except an overgrown puppy with snow on his mind. If Hal had had anyone to stand by him, I'd have turned and run home.

Once I'd recognized the hulk ahead of us, I slowed down again, even though the black form gave no sign of suspecting that anyone was following. No stops. No turns. No surreptitious glances over the shoulder. No one, I thought, was looking or listening for me, but with one hard shake of Rowdy's head, the unmistakable ring of dog tags could set that hulking form after us like an oversize Newfoundland intent on a belled kitten. I wished I'd had the foresight, before leaving home, to replace Rowdy's tag-hung leather collar with a soundless nylon choke, but it was too late. I didn't even have a training collar with me. I could probably have muffled the tags while I unbuckled the leather collar, but I had no replacement for it, and I wouldn't have turned him loose to dash into the traffic of Concord Avenue even if it were the only threat the night held. I ran my gloved left hand over his big head, partly to comfort myself, partly to tell him to stay calm and, I prayed, soundless.

Ahead of us was the darkest stretch of Concord Avenue, the block that runs by the long, wide fenced-in baseball field we'd have to pass before reaching the playground and, beyond the playground, the armory. Beyond the field, I knew, was the Tobin School, but its lights weren't on, and it appeared only as a form slightly darker than the field itself. Ahead, on the edge of the sidewalk, just before the playground, stood the little bus shelter. Shelter. A misnomer. Ambuscade. Suddenly, the sidewalk ahead was empty. Concord Avenue yawned emptily on my right. The deserted office building down the street offered not even the comfort of a single bright window. On my left, the chain link fence separated us from the field and offered no hiding, no escape. Had that lumbering figure slipped into the bus shelter? The field? The playground? Had my wool cap, with its brave row of sled dogs, deafened me, but not the listener, to a soft clink of tags?

I stopped, pressed Rowdy against the fence, and listened. My heart was jumping and pounding like a tethered sled dog. Rowdy's soft panting was the only other sound I heard. The light over the front door of the armory and a row of small floods along the side of the building shone hazily through the snow. What quirk of Cambridge politics, I wondered, had determined the absence of streetlights along this dark stretch of Concord Avenue? And the baseball field. Didn't the Little League have any clout? Hadn't anyone ever heard of night games?

Night games. That's what this was, a night game in the dark, and dark it was, darker, somehow, because of those dull little lights on the armory, darker than any snowless night thanks to the eerie pink glow the sky takes on when it snows here. Night vision, I thought. I've got to stop looking at the lights on the armory, the headlights of the cars, the sky. I have to stare into the blackness and let my eyes adapt, just the way I did when I was a child when we'd walk home from the store at night. After the brightness of the store, the road home was at first indiscernible. Creamsicles in hand, we'd pretend we were blind, groping our way along the edge of the blacktop, staring into the night, then gradually the sandy shoulders at the side of the road would appear, then trees, rocks, our own white sneakers. I sank my eyes into the blackness of the field and ran them over it toward the bus shelter and the playground, then back again.

The old trick worked. Was it rods or cones? Something in the retina. Rods. Shapes appeared. In the playground, somewhere near the dark mass of the climbing structure, something moved. I tugged softly on Rowdy's leash and stepped forward heel-first, then toe, then heel, then toe until we'd almost reached the cover of the bus shelter. With luck, we'd blend into it.

"Hey, buddy. Got something for you."

The voice was closer than I'd expected and loud with fake heartiness. Two shapes. Moving. Moving low down. Then a glint that almost pulled my eyes back toward the armory. The light from the floods on the side of the building had caught something out there near the climbing structure, something that reflected their light.

"Cold out here, huh, buddy? Thought you could use a little warming up." The voice was softer now, almost gentle. "Guys said you hadn't checked in tonight, and I said to myself, old Hal knows better ways to keep warm than that stew they dish out there. Old Hal doesn't want their stew. Do you, pal?"

Night vision. Mine was good now. Night games. Roger's game with Hal. I could see them now, and I could see Roger hand something to Hal, something that caught the light, a bottle. It had to be. I moved quickly to the far side of the bus shelter so I was flattened against it and almost in the playground. I'd always known that Hal was a gentleman. He raised the bottle jauntily toward Roger to offer his benefactor the first swig.

"It's all yours, pal," Roger said ungraciously, and he laughed, then started across the playground in my direction.

Hal lifted the bottle toward his mouth. I ran toward him and shouted, "No! Hal, it's me, Holly. Drop it! Don't drink it!"

I should have realized that I wasn't the first person who'd told Hal to quit drinking and that he'd know how to handle the injunction. He handled it in his usual way. He ran off into the blackness leaving Rowdy and me alone in the playground with Roger.

"You bitch," he said.

I took it as a compliment. That's how I was brought up.

"Thanks," I said. "But before you come any closer, there's something I have to tell you. I've got this code, and it says I've got to give fair warning. Try anything with me, and you'll put me in the hospital."

I'd overestimated him. Even in Cambridge, not everyone reads Spenser. He didn't say anything. He grabbed Rowdy's leash out of my hand, wrapped one arm around my head, and dragged me. His arm was across my face. I wasn't sure where we were going, but I was willing to bet it wasn't toward the armory. I couldn't breathe right, and I couldn't open my mouth to scream. Rowdy didn't make a sound. My neck was at an odd angle, and it hurt so much that I was almost relieved when he dumped me on the ground. I thought for a second that I had a chance to run for it, but I was wrong. The next moment, before I could yell, he was on top of me, pinning me to the snow with his weight. The moment after that, his solid gloved hand slammed down on my neck. I expected more blows, but looking up, I saw that he was busy with something in his hands, something shiny that jingled very quietly. I'd know that sound anywhere. A metal training collar. A choke collar. A choke chain. Lion's oversize training collar, too big for her. I could hear Rowdy moving, his tags clinking together. The next second, the chain slipped over my head, and Roger was standing above me, a leash in his hand, the leash fastened to the collar around my neck.

If I expected anything, I expected him to do to me what he'd done to his uncle, get it over fast, and take off. The ground was incredibly cold, and the snow had worked its way into my hair and around the icy chain. He kept the chain tight, but I could see that he was doing something—in fact, doing something with Rowdy, fastening the lead in his hand to Rowdy. The chain bit hard into my neck, cutting at my windpipe. I couldn't make a sound. With my good night vision, I watched him fumble with Rowdy's collar, and I watched him run ahead of Rowdy and pull hard.

"Mush!" he yelled.

The dope. Nobody says "mush" anymore. It's strictly Sergeant Preston stuff. You tell the dog to pull or go, not mush, but Rowdy wouldn't have understood that, either. He'd never been trained to pull, and, thank God, he didn't need any training to understand that the bastard was trying to murder me. As Roger yanked and stomped and bellowed at him to mush, Rowdy first held steady, legs straight and strong, then he backed up until he was standing over me. He was so close that I could watch him part his black lips and offer a ritual display of gleaming white teeth. He lowered his head a little, pulled back his ears, and through those big teeth, let loose a snarl more deep and loud than I'd ever heard before from any dog or any wolf. His hackles rose, and all over his great muscled body, the fur stood out, thick and silvery. Twice his normal size, he was a growling, shining menace.

His courage must have inspired me. I got one gloved hand to my neck, loosened the chain, and tried to scream for help, but nothing in my throat was working. All I could do was gasp for air. I thought I was going to pass out, but then, through the growling, I heard shouts that I at first mistook for my own. Loud, rough cries surrounded me, wet fur, hands, and, at last, light, the brightness of the armory entrance hall, a scratchy blanket making my cheeks itch, and faces, Gerry Pitts, John, and Hal. And Rowdy, licking my face and my raw neck.

Chapter 19

MOST of the blood came from fairly superficial cuts and scratches attributable to Roger Singer's predictable choice of a shoddy training collar. The rough metal loop had done the worst damage. Rowdy gave me the same first aid he'd have applied to himself. Even so, my neck may never look the same again.

Gerry's first aid consisted of forcing me to remain supine on an army cot under layers of green blankets. Some men have an unreasonable fear of blood. I tried to tell him that I wasn't suffering from hypothermia, but the words wouldn't come out. He misread Rowdy's scouring operation as vampirism, but I clung to Rowdy's collar and waved Gerry off when he tried to pull Rowdy away. Gerry might have succeeded if the lead had been fastened right, but it was still the way Roger had left it. He'd unbuckled the collar, slipped the collar through the loop on the lead that belongs in your hand, and rebuckled the collar.

I'm not sure how long I lay on the army cot wishing I could talk. Although it was probably only half an hour, it seemed longer, and the longer I lay there, the more helpless I felt, and the more helpless I felt, the more I wished that Rowdy had gone for Roger's throat. I was so angry that it was days before I realized that Rowdy couldn't have gone for Roger's throat without tightening the collar on mine. Rita later attributed my fury and my distorted sense of time to the peculiar nature of my early relationship with my parents, especially my mother. She maintained that my loss of voice was a hysterical reaction. According to Rita, words were what distinguished me from the other pups. Injured and mute, she claims, I lost my principal basis of competition with my psychological siblings, and I regressed to a state of diffuse infantile rage. When I told Rita that maybe she was right, since I'd never been so angry before, she threw me one of those psychotherapist smiles and said, "Ah, but you have. That's the point."

Just as I was starting to feel a little better, Kevin Dennehy and an ambulance crew arrived. Kevin's face showed touching and unwarranted alarm on my behalf. I had no intention of getting into the ambulance—no dogs allowed—but I couldn't think of any wordless way to say that I was fine except for my neck. Shaking my head yes or no sent great stabs of pain up to my head and down through my shoulders. I wrapped one hand around Rowdy's collar, pointed my other hand at the medics, looked straight at Kevin, and mouthed "No!"

"No dogs in the ambulance," he said. "Okay, but you're going to Mt. Auburn. Someone'll drive you. You and the dog can wait in the cruiser until they're ready for you."

Mrs. Dennehy thinks she's the real Christian in that family, but she's wrong. Even though I'd been right, I shouldn't have been so impatient with Kevin that day. He's intelligent as well as kind. He produced a pen and notebook.

"Pain in the neck," I wrote.

It was an apology. He likes bad puns. His eyes sparkled and he put a hand on my shoulder. I also wrote out Roger Singer's name and address and the message, "His dog."

"I hate to tell you," Kevin said, "but he's been there and gone."

On the way to Mt. Auburn, I tried sitting up in the back of the cruiser, but my neck hurt. I tried lying down. My neck still hurt but not quite so much. The uniformed cop at the wheel, one of Kevin's minions, looked about eighteen. I think I made him nervous. He was just a kid. Maybe he wasn't used to women with bleeding necks. Or maybe, it occurred to me, he was just afraid of dogs. At Mt. Auburn, we left Rowdy in the cruiser, and I checked in at the desk. The minion did the talking for me, and I filled in a form the nurse gave me. I wasn't dying, so there'd be a forty-minute wait, she said. An ambulance and another cruiser wailed in, and the minion spent the forty minutes with his colleagues in the second cruiser. Maybe they compared victims.

I stretched out on the back seat of the cruiser with Rowdy next to me on the floor. I rubbed his nose and dug my fingers into the thick fur around his head and neck. It was still snowing. As dogs go, malamutes are almost odorless, but even a malamute eventually perfumes an overheated car, especially if he's damp. Not everyone likes the aroma of a wet dog in a hot car, but I do. It helps me think. When I closed my eyes and held my head absolutely still, the pain wasn't bad. I made pictures on my closed eyelids and told myself a story. Here's how it went.

The story started years ago with the feud between those two scrappers, Frank Stanton and Margaret Robichaud. Year after year, they vied with one another for scores and ribbons and trophies and for position: chairman of this, head of that. Overall, Margaret won the competition in the ring, but she lacked Stanton's financial power, and she was a woman. He made big donations, established his informal library, and contributed fancy trophies. He was the aristocratic patron of the sport. By comparison, she was hired help. Stanton was, however, older than Margaret. As he aged and as his vision faded, she grew into the aspiring young wolf who sees the alpha male's power begin to wane. I could see them as they'd been at dog training only a few years ago, goading and taunting one another until Margaret, dominant bitch that she was, took up his challenge.

She'd gone to Janet Switzer, and she'd used her clout in the show world to buy the best pup Janet had, her great challenge to Stanton. As I saw it, that's when things started to go bad for her. She got what she paid for, King, the perfect malamute, intelligent, independent, and strong-minded, no one's toady. It was easy to imagine him as a pup, snapping at his lead, playing his tricks, refusing Margaret the submissive cooperation that, to her, meant obedience. I knew him, and I knew her. By the time he was nine months old, they must have been locked in such a battle of wills that his disappearance—nothing personal, just malamute wandering—was a shameful relief to her. In the meantime, when the club fired her, she also lost a major battle in her war with Stanton. By the time she talked to Ray and Bud, maybe she was eager to believe that King was dead.

Nameless and on the loose, her dog followed the end-of-summer traffic south from Maine to New Hampshire until, just over the Massachusetts border, he got lucky. The man whose chickens he killed, instead of shooting him as a wolf, caught him and, mistaking his breed, turned him over to the Siberian Rescue League. The Siberian people would have known that Bobbi would take him in. She did, and once she had him, his route to Stanton's was paved. Even if Dr. Stanton hadn't gone to her place for a meeting, she'd eventually have given him a call. She knew his dog had died and that he'd want another. She also knew that since he'd stopped going to shows, he might be willing to adopt a dog without papers. Stanton, I was sure, had taken one look at that gorgeous dog and seen the ultimate symbol of his victory over Margaret. From the moment the man with the chickens mistook a malamute for a Siberian, I realized, it was inevitable that Margaret's King would become Stanton's Rowdy, that he'd live on Appleton Street, a few blocks from Avon Hill.

Another part of the story also went back a long way. Roger, I thought, must have always considered himself his rich uncle's only relative. He was wrong, of course, as Dr. Stanton's lawyer knew and as Ron Coughlin was told. Really, we—the Cambridge Dog Training Club, the patrons of his library, dogs in general, his beloved Rowdy—were his natural heirs, but Roger, I guessed, hadn't known that. To Ron, who heard about the will but hadn't seen it, the legacy seemed almost too good to be true and too uncertain to count on. Roger, to guarantee his inheritance, wasted every Sunday on long, dreary dinners with his uncle, and just to make sure he was the good boy his uncle wanted him to be, he even got a dog, Lion, and made a pretense of training her. Although he didn't really train the dog, he grew fond of her in his own way. Like Rita, he didn't want to change the dog. He liked her the way she was. Consequently, when she started scratching and losing her fur, he took her to Dr. Draper, who eventually prescribed large doses of Valium, large not only because the dog was a Newfoundland but also because Dr. Draper, approaching retirement, was less cautious about tranquilizers than a young vet would have been and habitually wrote generous prescriptions anyway. Maybe the Valium worked, or maybe something else did. When Lion recovered, plenty of Valium was left.

In the meantime, the dog was hospitalized, and her stay at the hospital coincided with Dr. Stanton's trip to Chicago to receive his award. Since Roger was going to house-sit anyway, as he always did, and since Lion was in the hospital, he dog-sat as well. Dope that he was, he let Rowdy run loose. Rowdy found his skunk, and Roger's efforts to deodorize Rowdy showed him something his uncle's vision was too weak to reveal: the tattoo. He traced the number to Margaret, and he was bright enough to see that there was no longer any need to wait for his inheritance. He extorted regular sums from his uncle, who assumed, as Roger intended, that his tormentor was his old enemy, Margaret Robichaud.

That was as far as I got. The minion startled me when he opened the door of the cruiser.

"Miss Winter, they're ready for you," he said.

A resident swabbed me off in a more sanitary but less healing fashion than Rowdy had already done, made me turn my head, ordered X rays, told me I was lucky I could still breathe, prophesied that I'd feel worse in the morning, and finally sent me home with some wonderful painkillers.

I did feel worse in the morning. I took more painkillers. Even though it was Saturday, Mrs. Dennehy brought me some vegetarian imitation of chicken soup. Rita tried to take Rowdy for a walk, but after he dragged her down the block in pursuit of the cocker spaniel that he loathed, she gave up and hauled him home. I slept all afternoon. Without my knowledge or permission, Rita called Steve's clinic, got the number of his hotel in Philadelphia, and told him what had happened. She also phoned Buck for me and passed me the news that he'd finally reached Jim Chevigny, who'd made a couple of calls and confirmed my hunch that Buck hadn't been the first person to check on that AKC registration number.

Kevin dropped in, deposited a pot of purple chrysanthemums on my nightstand, blushed, drank a Bud, and told me some things about Dr. Stanton's finances that I hadn't known before. He also told me that Roger, Lion, and Roger's personal computer were gone.

"I told you he was the one who'd go for diskettes," I said. Mostly, however, I acted more gracious to Kevin than I usually do. Kevin's only problem is that he still misses his old dog.

By the time Steve arrived, I was up and dressed, and my voice was starting to strengthen. According to Rita, that's proof of the hysterical nature of my muteness, since my neck and throat were even more swollen than they were the night before. In lieu of flowers, Steve brought a bouquet of Old Mother Hubbard dog biscuits. How special is this guy? How many men know that the way to a woman's heart is through her dog's stomach?

After I told Steve the same story I'd told myself in the back of the cruiser, we finished it together.

"Roger made two big mistakes about Stanton," I croaked. "He overestimated how much Stanton could or would pay, and he underestimated the guy's guts. He must have figured that Stanton had a bigger income than he did or that he could tap the principal, which he couldn't, at least not without raising a lot of questions." Ever since I talked to Millie, I'd wondered whether Stanton was hurting for money, but I hadn't known the rest until Kevin told me. Kevin, of course, had interviewed Stanton's lawyer.

"And the old guy did have a lot of guts," Steve said. "He paid up, but the whole thing had a big impact. Everyone says he was looking sick. You remember? You told me. You said that the night he died, you noticed he was looking better than usual, the way he used to look. He'd decided to act."

"Right. And when he thought he was paying Margaret, it must have nearly killed him."

"Maybe Roger thought it would," Steve said.

"Until he saw the appointment book. You know what he saw there. The appointment with the lawyer. The appointment with Margaret. Roger never thought Stanton would go to Margaret, and, of course, if he had, that would have blown everything. Stanton might not have believed her at first, but eventually, he'd have had to, and he certainly wouldn't have paid any more."

"And once the thing was out in the open," Steve said, "Stanton would've traced it all to Roger sooner or later, and even if Stanton hadn't decided to prosecute, there goes the inheritance or what Singer thinks is his inheritance."

"And he's got to act fast, before his uncle sees Margaret."

Steve agreed. "Or the lawyer. So he ties Lion to the tree, waits for Stanton, grabs the leash he knows will be there, does him in, and hustles back for the dog."

"Which Hal has been patting."

"Which Hal has been patting," Steve said. "And he sees Hal there."

"Maybe. Or maybe he only figures that out later. You want to get the straight story out of Hal?"

He didn't bother answering that. "And he figures with the uncle dead, he gets the dog."

"Jesus. And pretty soon, an accident happens. No more dog, no more tattoo, no more evidence. A dog gets hit by a car, dies, and who checks its thigh for a tattoo? And even if someone does, so what? Speaking of which, that explains why Rowdy's shots were in Stanton's records even though he hadn't been to Dr. Draper. You know what I think happened? Time comes for his shots, and Roger doesn't want Dr. Draper looking closely."

"And," Steve said, "Stanton didn't drive anymore, so Roger volunteered, and he drove Rowdy around and brought him home."

"But he gambles that Rowdy stays healthy. If not, Stanton and Dr. Draper could have got together. Stanton would have said Rowdy'd had his shots, and Dr. Draper would have told him that Rowdy hadn't been in."

As Steve pointed out, it wasn't really a big gamble. Dr. Draper might have thought he'd forgotten to make a note in Rowdy's record, or Stanton could have thought that Dr. Draper's memory was slipping.

"So he sees me at the match, and he sees that Rowdy's all fluffy after his bath."

"That's part of it," Steve said. "He knows you're Buck Winter's daughter. You call the AKC, or Daddy does, and you don't just trace the number, you maybe also find out that other people have been asking about it, and you find out that one of the people wasn't Stanton."

"Plus he must have known I'd go after the papers. Everyone knows I show my dogs, so if I didn't know something already, I'd find out before too long. That's why he had the Valium with him. And after that, I was in the hospital, and he couldn't get to me. He must have been stunned when nothing happened. I mean, he must have expected me to figure out that Rowdy was Margaret's, and he must have expected me to tell everyone. If he'd been smart, he would have realized that he had me right where he'd had Stanton."

Steve disagreed. "He would've known you couldn't pay all that much, but he did expect you to make the connection with the tattoo and tell Kevin about it. In fact, when you didn't, that's when he sent the letter. It was too late to stop you from figuring out whose dog you had, and the police didn't suspect him of killing his uncle, mostly because he didn't inherit anything . . ."

"A nasty shock."

"Obviously. So Margaret Robichaud was all set up to take the blame for his uncle's murder, and he tried to speed things up and strengthen the case against her."

"I get it," I said. "Once Ron told that story about the skunk, Roger got really scared. The letter was one thing. I mean, that was sort of a sensible way to deflect everyone's suspicions to Margaret. But ransacking my place and leaving the fur? That just wasn't Margaret. It was a stupid thing to do."

Rita later told me that we were wrong. Leaving the fur, she said, wasn't just stupid. *Overdetermined* was her word for it. That fur was like the coat of Margaret's dogs, but, as I'd sensed, it was also like my own hair. On the surface, Roger was trying to incriminate Margaret. According to Rita, he was also unconsciously doing what I'd suspected and what had scared me: marking my bed with a symbol of violence against me. "You'd rejected him," she said. "It was revenge, symbolic rape."

"I wonder," I said to Steve, "whether he could have seen us with Hal, or whether it was when Hal ran away after class."

"He was probably panicky by then anyway," Steve said. "He'd expected to get Margaret, and it didn't work. Everything was still open. He was so panicked, he had to do something. Shutting Hal up was the obvious immediate thing to do."

"Only I wandered in."

"You have to admit," he said, "it would have been a fitting end for you. If Rowdy hadn't turned protective."

"I've been thinking it over," I said. "I'm not all that sure he was protecting me. It's just possible that he thought Roger wanted to give him another bath."

Chapter 20

"HIRAM Walker apricot brandy," Kevin announced. "It's what we used to buy for the girls when I was a kid."

It was early on Monday evening. We'd picked up dinner from the Colonel Sanders on the corner of Walden Street and Mass. Ave., and we both had our elbows on my kitchen table. Kevin likes their mashed potatoes and gravy. He believes in carbohydrate loading. My voice had returned to normal, and my neck didn't hurt quite so much anymore.

"No relation to Johnnie," I said. "Laced with?"

"Undiluted, unadulterated," said Kevin. "Pure Hiram Walker."

He'd been telling me about Roger, who was arrested that morning near Barre, Vermont. Sitting in a snowdrift at the side of Route 89, he'd been cradling Lion's giant, lifeless head in his lap and crying, or that's what the troopers told Kevin. Roger was driving his own car, which hadn't been spotted because he'd exchanged license plates with some neighbors (in fact, the quarrelsome couple with the golden), who hadn't noticed the switch. When he stopped by the side of the highway to exercise Lion, so to speak, she apparently slipped her collar and ran into the path of a semi. The driver, who pulled over, radioed the troopers. A cruiser was there within a few minutes, and it didn't take the troopers long to match the crying man with the big black dog to the description that had been sent out. I felt really bad about Lion. She was a love. You can't always read a person's character from his dog's, or vice versa.

Then Kevin told me that I'd be glad to know my old friend Hal was just fine.

"You mean I could've let him go ahead and drink it, then? It wasn't even poisoned?"

"Polished off half the bottle on his way to the armory," Kevin said, "and lived to tell about it, more or less."

"So I've sacrificed half the skin on my neck for nothing?"

"In my opinion," he said, "what Roger had in mind was a sort of premedication. If you look at Pace, he's no lightweight. It'd be a lot easier to get the chain on him if he was tanked up."

"So the collar was meant for him?"

"In my opinion," Kevin said.

"Has Roger said?"

"He's said zip shit."

"So where had he been?"

"At a Holiday Inn."

I told you they're great about dogs.

"There are a couple of things I still don't understand," I said. "First of all, what did he do with the money? He lived in a dump. He drove some little Chevy. I don't get it."

"There's nothing to get. He had a lot of cash on him."

"And the kid? The one I saw with him?"

"He was a regular of hers. Mother picked her up yesterday, took her home to Chelmsford. She'll be back in a week."

"I guess that's all you could do," I said. It was a feeble thing to say, but what could he have done? "So tell me about Margaret Robichaud. Where did the money come from all of a sudden? Did you find that out?"

"Brother's widow died."

"Bill Lytton?"

"Mrs. Shirley Lytton. Worshipped the dead husband, never remarried. No kids. Her family's loaded. She died and left the bundle to his sister, who built a dog palace."

My mail arrived at five o'clock. In Cambridge, you're lucky if it gets here at all and if it's not someone else's. There was an oversize white envelope with a return address in Greensboro, North Carolina. Inside were the premium lists and entry blanks for two shows. They were both in Massachusetts, not North Carolina, which is just the address of the show superintendent. The one in Woburn offered a trophy for the highest-scoring Alaskan malamute in obedience. The Novice B judge for that one was Eileen Bernstein, who knows good handling when she sees it.

I put on a fresh turtleneck, a corduroy jumper, dressy boots, my good woolen coat, and a pair of gloves that Rowdy hadn't unraveled. For a touch of bravado, I pulled on the sled dog hat, but I left Rowdy home. I didn't plan to be gone long. Avon Hill is fancier than the corner of Appleton and Concord, but, geographically speaking, it's nearby.

Margaret was not, of course, expecting me. When she came to the door, some of her hair was escaping from its usual swirl, her lipstick wasn't fresh, and she had a run in one of her stockings. The dogs must all have been in their palace. I didn't see or hear them the whole time I was there, but that wasn't for very long.

"I need to talk to you," I said. She still hadn't let me in.

"Holly," she said, "how are you? I was so distressed to hear what happened. Are you all right?"

"It was nothing," I said. "I'm fine. May I come in?"

She led me into the gold-carpeted study where we'd sat before.

"I want to have a little talk about a malamute," I said. I leaned back in the chair and tried to look relaxed. "A big male with a registration number tattooed way down on his inner thigh. WF818769. Does that ring any bells?"

I stared at her like a border collie eyeing an errant sheep.

"King died," she said coldly.

"Roy and Bud Rogers took in a dog that died. That dog had blue eyes."

"I don't know what you're talking about."

"I'm talking about my dog," I said. "Rowdy. Frank Stanton's dog, my dog. Yukon King, the Wonder Dog. Remember him? He's such a wonder dog that he's led more than one life. I want his registration certificate, and I want him transferred to me. Now."

She laughed. "Keep him," she said magnanimously. "Show him, if you want. There'll be plenty of fun matches in the spring. Or get an ILP number."

"No," I said. "I've come for his papers."

"What a silly girl you are," she said. "King died. Everyone knows that."

"The tattoo is proof," I said. "And if it weren't, don't you think Janet Switzer knows her own dogs?"

"To whom do you intend to show this proof? The AKC? Go ahead. Return him, and I'll thank you in public. You think I don't have room for him?"

"I know you have room for him. I also know something else: that you've learned a lot about dogs in the last year. He must have been a pretty wild puppy, but you've learned what to do about wild puppies, haven't you?"

She looked blank.

"*You* know," I added. "Puppies that get up when they're supposed to stay down?"

"One of my dogs fell asleep in the ring. It happens, you know."

"To high-strung young goldens," I said, "whose handlers haven't quite figured out how much Valium is too much."

"You're making something of nothing."

I bluffed. What else could I do? "Jim Chevigny won't think so. He has questions already, you know. Or maybe you don't know. A lot of people out there have answers to those questions, and I've heard some of them. I talk to a lot of people. It's part of my job. Do you have any idea how many people would just love to see an official inquiry? People are talking now, and, believe me, once Chevigny starts asking the right questions, there goes your good standing with the AKC. You'll have to find another hobby, won't you?"

She wiped her mouth with the back of her hand. It was an uncharacteristic gesture. She's usually quite ladylike.

"There is no truth in those rumors," she said.

I knew she was lying, but I was prepared to let her save face. All that really held her back, I was sure, was the prospect of everyone seeing Rowdy's real name in the show catalogs. Even if she transferred ownership to me, some people would recognize Rowdy's real name in the catalogs, and they'd ask her a lot of awkward questions.

"If you're worried about the name," I said, "you must have forgotten who my father is. He can fix it."

The point, which Margaret understood immediately, is that it's easier to get the pope to beatify you than it is to get the AKC to change a dog's name. Margaret's face had no expression. She stood up, walked calmly to her desk, opened a drawer, and pulled out a manila folder. From the folder she removed a slip of paper. It was white with a violet border. She signed it on the back, replaced it in the folder, and handed me the whole thing.

"There's a four-generation pedigree there," she said. "It might interest you."

"It will," I said.

She showed me to the door, and I thanked her. "You know, Margaret, I admire you," I said. "You're a good loser, better than I expected."

Although Buck did speed things up at the AKC, a month passed before the new registration certificate arrived. I put it in the pocket of my parka, and Steve and I walked Rowdy down Appleton Street toward Brattle. New snow was starting to cover the dirty drifts on the lawns and the icy ruts in the roads. Dr. Stanton's house had stood empty since Millie moved to Florida, but someone, probably Ron Coughlin, had shoveled the sidewalk. The Cambridge Dog Training Club was still negotiating with the neighborhood, and we didn't yet know what we'd be able to do with the house.

"You know," I said, "I don't believe Roger just assumed he'd inherit everything. I have a feeling that Stanton led him on. You didn't really know Stanton, and I didn't know him all that well, but he wasn't such a nice man. You didn't see him with Margaret Robichaud, but he never missed the chance to get in a dig. I think he did the same thing with Roger, only in reverse, if you see what I mean. He let him believe it was all coming to him."

"So what are we doing here?"

"He was good to Rowdy," I said. "That counts, too."

We turned right on Brattle Street and followed it until the merge with Mt. Auburn. Across the street was the Mt. Auburn Cemetery, which is conveniently close to the hospital without actually being visible to the patients. It's a famous bird-watching spot. It's also notable for its elaborate monuments, including some statues of people's pets. It seemed to me bizarre that Dr. Stanton's body was resting in a place that didn't allow dogs unless they were carved out of marble. It was more than bizarre. It was wrong.

If you ever decide to sneak a flesh-and-blood dog into the Mt. Auburn Cemetery, I'd suggest one of the toy breeds. The high metal fence that surrounds the cemetery has a few spots where you could slide in a papillon or a Pekinese. You could tuck a Chihuahua in your pocket and hope he didn't bark while you walked through the gates. An Alaskan malamute is no toy, in any sense of the word. I think we succeeded mostly because new snow was just beginning to cover the old gray snow on the ground, so Rowdy's coat gave him perfect camouflage. Also, he practically never barks. Steve walked on one side of him, I walked on the other, and we slipped in as fast as we could.

I'd already scouted out Dr. Stanton's grave, which was at the far end of the cemetery. If I ever have as much money as Dr. Stanton did, I'll order one of those marble dogs. In fact, I'll make sure that I eventually rest under a whole pack of life-size golden retrievers. I'd like to go out the way I came in, the eighteenth puppy.

Dr. Stanton's monument was just a granite stone with hi name and the dates of his birth and death. Steve stood behi it and took off his hat. The snow made his hair curl even m than usual. He had a foolish grin on his face. He wasn't taking it as seriously as I was. I brought Rowdy to heel about ten feet in front of the stone.

"This is so corny," Steve said.

I just said, "So what?"

"Ready?" he asked. The AKC requires judges to ask that.

"Ready," I said.

We went through the whole Novice routine. For the last exercise, I stood right in front of the stone so Rowdy faced the inscription.

"Down," I said, and I left him there for the full three minutes.

When I released him at the end of the long down, he bounced in the air, landed, and shook himself. That's just what I want for myself, a big dog dancing on my grave.

On our way out, one of the guards spotted us, but I hollered an apology, and we took off across Mt. Auburn Street and down Brattle like naughty kids. In a block, we slowed down, and Steve kissed me.

"You know," I said, "there's still one thing that bothers me. I thought we were going to find out about Antarctica, about the massacre."

"It's too long ago."

"Maybe," I said. "But I wanted to know. I still do. I wanted to get that bastard."

"He's probably dead."

"He's probably alive and well and living in Argentina."

"And what would you do if you found him? There isn't any Nuremberg for crimes against dogs."

"There isn't one *yet*," I said.

"He wasn't court-martialed, was he? It wasn't a criminal act."

It was in my book.